I0749297

SISTERS

Also by John Fraser
and published by
AESOP Modern Fiction:

Animal Tales
Black Masks
Blue Light / Starting Over
The Case
Down from the Stars
Enterprising Women
Happy Always
Hard Places
An Illusion of Sun
The Magnificent Wurlitzer
Medusa
Military Roads
The Observatory
The Other Shore
The Red Bird
The Red Tank
Runners
Soft Landing
The Storm
Thirty Years
Three Beauties
Wayfaring

SISTERS

John Fraser

AESOP Modern Fiction
Oxford

AESOP Modern Fiction
An imprint of AESOP Publications
Martin Noble Editorial / AESOP
28a Abberbury Road, Oxford OX4 4ES, UK
www.aesopbooks.com

First edition published by AESOP Publications

www.johnfraserfiction.com

A catalogue record of this book is available from the British Library.

First edition 2017, revised 2024

ISBN: 978-1-910301-38-8

THEY'RE THREE SISTERS – that's evocative . . . they could be Russian – frustrated, horrible or anorexic.

None of those.

If you've a childhood in a sect – it's a big room that gets smaller and smaller when you've closed the door on it, but it's still your birth-room. The travail's a memory that stays. Lots of early things, left inside you.

One, works in a white coat: super conductors, looking for something that lasts for ever – it's what the cat already has, if you don't think it'll ever end, you can remember everything (or forget it) and it's all good or bad, and it always has exactly the same value, the same weight – a kindness or a kick. A cat lives so. Nothing is wiped away or buried. It's all yours. But you keep schtum about it, like a cat.

Another sister – does everything she wants, just ricketing around, always reacting, attracting, repelling – the kind you'd want to see on screen, you'd want to go to bed with her – but then – you want to go to bed with almost anyone. She discriminates somewhat, you don't.

A biking accident – her guy, the pilot, lobotomised . . . sweet and gentle for ever, useless but courteous. She, paralysed wholly. For ever, a lump unleavened on a narrow bunk. No story there.

The third's gone, looking after an older man's kids. Some sex, probably, but not shown.

So – back to the first. Who's to tell who's story? She's been hunted. Usually, it's the hunter who's remorseful. Or proud. Not this time. This hunter isn't into storytelling.

Doctor Gritt, her boss – takes his crew up to his camp, his cottage in the wilds. It's a training, he sells it as a favour, fun.

'No, it's a bore,' she says. She won't go – she's wrong, a mistake.

She's always been a hard one. Trained to be a surgeon – but . . . all those poor animals, cut up in exam rooms – no, better lead a battle. . . 'Everyone cut off their index finger – show we're for nature, and not nurture. . .' That's what she said – the only one so expert with the scalpel. Off it goes – no pointing, prodding, ever more – and one career she'll never have.

'Thoreau,' she shouts out to the Prof, 'says a free person is one who speaks her mind.'

'That's so,' the guy says, in a sweat, 'if that is all you want. But with that face-veil – you're anonymous.'

'A book,' says Masha – that's her name, no secret there . . . it could be an invention, though. 'It has no face. Its covers hide its thought. But once inside it – you speak quite free. That is my veil . . . a book. My freedom.'

'It's crap,' the lecturer shouts. 'What's in books – it may be free, or not. But there are maybe more important things that contents can be – or else are not.'

'Well,' says Masha. 'True. The voice is rather limited. Quite individual. That freedom – well, so what?'

'That's heavy thoughts,' the guy says. 'I'm only here to lecture on eternity, and some machine to take us there. A conductor – like on a bus, time back. You can't critique what you believe, you have to take a stand. That way you're free, and then, maybe – you're not. . .'

She's wondered what her town looks like, when it's been pounded – that cheap cement back into dust, ready for another round. The people not like her, and those she doesn't like – laid out, quiet, carried to the holy ground. . . Now, she has her chance to see it all, the end.

It's a kind of prayer, she says, running down the beach: and God can fix it. But He doesn't calm the waters, nor adjust the motor on the dinghy, nor glue her shoe soles gaping on the long walk. He's non-proven, for her. She doesn't wear the veil when she's with Doctor Gritt, her boss – and doesn't want to bond with him, his ego.

'You must be from Dagestan,' says Doctor Gritt. 'An Eden. Too bad you don't like nature.'

She's not from there – she'd quite like to be. She doesn't wear the veil – most don't here. A veil's a veil a veil. A *persienne.* It's not a voice – it's silent, and you're silent too, behind it. It isn't her, but not much is, except herself. With Doctor Gritt, she has herself: that's a disadvantage too.

'Look, Masha,' says Doctor Gritt, 'I don't care where you're from. But – I see in you extremes. Are you by chance, Masha, an extremist?'

'Oh yes, Doctor Gritt,' says Masha, sweetly, 'I'm an extremist. Everyone around me has extreme existences, has done extreme things. You could call them radical, when they've time to think. I've worn the veil. I've thrown it off. Don't underestimate me, Doctor Gritt.'

'Oh,' he says, 'I'd not do that. The point is – our research – is done by teams. Teamwork is something you don't like.'

'You're obsessed with this,' says Masha. 'Teams, bands, gangs, sects. My clothes – once, they make the point. Just once: then it's all changed. You change, your clothes are changed, they're past. Tattoos – they remember those, because they're on your skin. Skin's remembered – it's big and wrapped around. Your face – is not memorable. My skin's pristine. My face – is like the others. . . I've always had people round – but not a team. A team's to make the money, lots of it. Not for me. The people I know, they'd like an easy life: you do only what's expected – don't try to innovate. Our work. . . A conductor, super? An Über and an Ober? A machine eternal, cool for ever? Soft firm hands. . . I don't believe it. If you make it, and the money that goes with, I'm not interested. Someone'll be on your heels; some luck, they get there first.'

'It's you who's looking for eternity,' says Doctor Gritt. 'For me – it's just preserving energy that's not squandered. Not stasis, not perpetual immobility. Without an index, Masha, you're no use. What an impulse! If you'd cut off your great toes, you'd fall over endlessly – but I'd have found a chair for you. Without a point, a pointer, there's left for you – only the mind's life. How the world seems. No thing stands out, it's all worth equally. Happenstance – I'm sure you've seen the cats – that's how they live. There is no focus, resolution, no here, no there. If it had been your thumb – no hitching rides – that's dangerous anyway. Nothing to distinguish you from thumbless jaguars – except you don't run fast, and you've no tail. But – the finger. Remember, how it points, it wrote, "Weighed in the balance . . . wanting." We all want, but, Masha, at a glance, you're wanting! If I make a parcel – I can't ask you to block the string. No pen to hold, no brush, even to pick your nose. . .'

'I know,' says Masha. 'It's half a tragedy.'

'Another hand,' the Doctor says. 'A spare . . . it's not the same. That missing length . . . castration! A void – you'll gyre your life around it. . . I took you on – I pitied you, and felt sorry for myself. Now – you're fired – I feel pity for myself – but, Masha, most problems can't be solved. Sometimes fighting and a massacre will help. For most hard places, it's time, dissatisfaction, generations of bad dreams. You're now in one of those. No one can help you – anyway, you didn't ask for help. Don't be surprised when that help doesn't come: you're self-inflicted. The mind, Masha, the mind. See how it unfolds, like paper flowers in water. Or in gin. The choice is yours. Maybe you'll hallucinate, adopt a child, turn to religion, or away.'

'It could have been a heel, an eye, my wound,' says Masha. 'You're not from here, dear Doctor. Do you have identity? Or just a personality? And do you care? I could have been in China – they move about so much, and miss their mothers, get beaten, fired, and beaten up again, fall in with bandits, or the bus . . . topples down the unkempt hillside . . . so, here I stand. I can't stand elsewhere.'

'I told you – you've your toes,' the Doctor says.

'You'll walk and walk.'

*

It's better so. Already a flight, a revolution exploded in its box, armies from everywhere to sort it out . . . and then a job, what luck! its heavy body lying on her, grunting and getting fat and bald. Kids arriving like the witch's curse, around the doorframe, there they stand with greedy eyes and rickety legs. . . Most people take a Russian name, when they get out – the Russians don't just hit, they win.

Many people live in hard states, really hard. Stalin without Stalin. Without the mission, just camps and prisons of every kind. I had all those people round me. Sleeping close, too close, hands in my sack. You need a mission, or it's just all scoundrels and ghosts.

No, Masha thinks, I've lived one life right through. I need find something else.

*

'I envy you, Masha, leaving the team,' Delia says. 'I would too – but I've no country to go back to.'

'No one can win the war back home, and no one can

be defeated,' Masha says. 'The people should move out. Just armies. Armies are inexhaustible. My sisters – one died for love, the other – entombed for family. That leaves me free. I'll stay. I'll roam. I'll look for somewhere enchanted, and a way to keep the others out.'

'They'll make you do the therapy,' says Delia. 'In case you are extreme. They'll draw it out: your brain – comes tumbling down your nose.'

'I'm free,' says Masha. 'If I want, I'll choose my chains and snap them on, and hear them! Clank!'

'It's not a joke,' says Delia. 'No one laughs round here.'

*

There's an inflection here – moresques twined round the voice, the orange fruit, inside it's – red. The passion flowers, the bignonias – red. Orange. Depends on distance – orange, red or pink. The old man says, 'It's frightening – you're not aware your brain has gone – it's like a puzzle dropped and broken, the pieces higgled here and there, under a chair, a carpet fringe. You scrabble round – what was the picture? What got broke – it didn't signify a lot when it was whole, but now – it's crumbs.'

'Yes,' Masha says, not interested: 'I'd heard. Another

fear arrives when the past has gone, and there's no future left.'

It's hot, there's sea, white light all over – it's like the beach where Caravaggio ran after the ship with all his pictures – died exhausted. . . A story, that. Invention; a naughty boy is dead, another makes a lie about what happened.

'If there's a picture, old man – it's always breaking up. The scenes are stacked high in our heads, ready to topple. War, hunger, chased out, held fast so's to experience unwanted dirty tricks – do people go through this, and then they must behave bad, as a response, infection? No, it can't be so – they're here, therefore they can't have had their guts ripped out, or else we shouldn't see them. They've heard it, seen it on a screen, watched it, the final battle, run away. . . It's an excuse for them to struggle harder, so's they can survive, and so that others can't. They steal and elbow, take your name and document and food: – of course. Anybody would. Saints can't be saintly all the time – they must defend their haloes, or they would be nicked.' Masha doesn't say all this, she thinks it, how it would be wasted on this amnesiac old guy, who's seen it all but now forgotten, anyway, it's late – though even when it's early, it's irrelevant.

The distant pink, the red, the orange, sometimes sweet, and sometimes fire and flame.

It's an experience, she thinks, sitting here, no questions, no destination, no special anxiety, no empty future to fill up.

*

'What's it like', she's asked, 'being you? All those experiences! Just say, in your own words, and we would broadcast it.'

There's a purpose for sure, behind this, but it's not hers.

'Do you pay me?' she asks.

'No,' says the guy doing the interview: 'It's against the ethic. But I guess there is expenses. . .'

'I have those too,' says Masha. 'It's my words, but it's your purpose, my expenses, your cash.'

'Yes,' says the guy. 'But you must suppose you're interesting, or we'll talk to someone else.'

'I could make something up,' says Masha. 'That'll be interesting. For me, as well.'

They find someone else – Masha doesn't care.

*

Delia has a sister too – Alina. They perch in their tree-house, drinking a red Corvo.

'Masha's drifted far from the shore,' says Delia. 'We've put gender behind us, but there's still the culture. It has its rules and codes. Men, women. . . One day, we'll all converge on something in the middle, between those old men, old women, when they're gone. Or – not the middle: just splaying out all over, keen or indifferent. Maybe we'll be dead. Maybe it'll come, our something, hybrid, or vengeful, and we shan't notice. Sex or faith. Or the bell jar, the antheap, where we all do our things. Maybe it's here now, and Masha's fighting ghosts. . .'

'Maybe she's a ghost,' Alina says. 'There's nothing else for her to do – she's the sheep who smells the knife and runs. You don't want to find another flock, another hypocrite, a shepherd who saves you from the wolves and gifts you to the pigs.'

'What comes after,' Delia says. 'After everyone, is monsters. That's the issue: they have codes and rules. A solitary monster – that you'd recognise. Lurking in the woods. not finding one virgin in the village – famished and frustrated. And then – there's the crowd of them – the devils. A master of the dance, a Mephisto? – we don't believe in one alone. Satan – he converged. He was male and female, had a culture. He must have had a team.

Remember the Damnation – there was a bunch of creatures, named, that spurred them on, on to the abyss. And yet, that great devil was progressive. Draining the Pontine marsh – that was his plan, and then she – the soprano – touched his female part: – he lets Margherita off the drop.'

'Well,' says Alina. 'About Masha. Is she a monster too? She's been dead once. . .'

'Oh, absolutely,' Delia says. 'Stay clear of her. Everybody does – she's learned her script, and no one else can speak a line. She hides behind the trees – but roars.'

'Another one that roars,' Alina says, 'is Doctor Gritt. Wants his troupe of females. The best thing would be – they don't lie down to have their kids in hospitals: they're on all fours and drop them in the bush; and if the offspring stand – they'll go into flourishing trades, and marry lovely herbivores.'

'Well, Alina,' Delia says, kissing her sister on the nose. 'We want none of that, do we? And if the soldiers come – the leaves will hide us. . . We mustn't throw the bottles down – that's a big giveaway in life.'

It starts to rain – on the leaves, it's like raisins or almonds dropped on paper – it doesn't get to them. 'Masha says you're supposed to want peace, when there's war all round and war inside. She doesn't want the peace, she says. It's a con, what you're supposed to want, and how to get there,' Alina says. 'She needs some work – maybe something not invented yet, or something obsolete.'

'No,' Delia says. 'She doesn't want to work. It's enough to say you do. You don't.'

The tree rocks – 'We should have kept our tails,' says Alina. 'That way, you cling. I've an aunt, no mother. You've a mother and no aunt – and yet we're sisters. Kiss me, Delia,' and Delia leans to her, but doesn't kiss.

'Doctor Gritt is evil,' Delia says. 'And we are geniuses. Masha too – especially. We should come down now, come to earth. . . They catch quails with sultanas, like under this mulberry tree. They can't tell fruit from fruit – like us. We're quails, Alina, but no one's going to catch us.'

'They catch Sultanas with the quails,' Alina says. 'No one's catching me! The Sultan fell off his elephant, got trampled on his wedding day . . . in recognition, I'll eat no animal flesh. Maybe organs though. . .'

'Doctor Gritt says his device will last for ever – but it won't. It'll last till we're not here, and can't bear witness. Do you think souls last for ever, Alina?' Delia asks. 'Stars don't, and they used to say they were the souls, the old, old souls of. . .'

'Monsters!' Alina says. 'Certainly – monsters. Like Doctor Gritt – circling round up there in turgid galaxies, waiting for his Plouf! and – there! he's gone.'

'Doctor Gritt – he has sisters too,' says Delia. 'Two stayed back, in his village. They have traditional lives, they toil with their traditional hands, digging the world we lost and long for but at all costs hope we can avoid. . . You guess what their deaths will be, and their descendants' too. I danced the *zouk* with Doctor Gritt – it's the raunchiest! You wave your haunches – like ibexes. . . He came on too strong – I accused him. . . But he said the sister who came with him to Germany, she was big in arty circles. . . If he fired me, he said, he'd put in a word with her. She's called Linda. Be Linda – that's how strong!'

'He represents the fleeting victory, ephemeral ascendancy, of power,' says Alina, solemnly. 'But the *zouk* and him – it throws a different light. . .'

'I shan't go to his camp again,' says Delia, 'I promise, Alina dearest.'

'You should tell him,' Alina says. 'Some moon moths are born for sex and death – but they've no mouths. Those aren't essential. They don't eat, just procreate – so, learn the lesson, Doctor Gritt!'

*

Delia says, 'Doctor Gritt told me, "You're talking about stagnation. Our work, our science, gets us out of it. You're stuck there, Delia! We start from what is stagnant – maybe in the end, that's the state that we produce. It's what you need, you want, you get, if you have things that last, go on for ever. Energy that doesn't dissipate. It seems dynamic when you seek – but in the end – it's steady-state. . . For ever – nullity." That's fine. Logical. A paradox: I like it. It's him that I don't care for.'

'You're narrow, Delia,' says Alina. 'Though I don't mind.'

'He says,' says Delia, '"I love giving the traumatised some hope. A job. There are so many of them, who've lived their lives right through, and still they walk among us. The work we do, our experiments, those white coats we wear, ethereal. Eternity – the point, the value, must be clear."'

'I told you,' says Alina. 'He's arrogant. A turkey cock. A hungry feast will come to him!'

'Gritt is therapy,' Delia says. 'Whatever your trauma – whatever that may mean – if you don't follow him, you've no hope, no help. The conductor: – it's the future for us all. A future more stable than the past.'

'Oh Delia,' Alina says, 'don't exaggerate! Masha will find another job, where you don't need to point a finger, nor to press a tab.'

'People like Masha,' Delia says, 'who've seen deaths, been threatened, been an inch away – they must be cured, turned around – or else they're barren, rotten, like the others they were with. Some were robbers, others linked arms with her – it's all the same, you're all scrambling up the stair. . . When you've climbed the tower, survived – you don't look up: that would be logical, but no, at the top – you look down. To where you were. You fear the fall: not that you might fly. So it is with her. That's the lesson. You look up, although there's nothing there. Her history – it's all around, in heads and screens – truths from every angle, big and small, partial and shaky. . . Forget all that. You fix on what Masha has become, submerging in her history for ever. No! You mustn't stay behind, earthbound. She isn't what's she's been. You must climb the tower, keep on, ever upward – look high into the void. . . You, she, we. . .'

She laughs. It isn't humorous.

'Leaves, my dear,' Alina says. 'If you're lucky, you see leaves. A sole, a pad, a paw, that skitters up, a life higher than you'll ever be.'

They look up at the tree, the worms that prowl among the fruit. 'Oh the lovely lassies', you might think.

'When you get off work,' Alina says, 'we'll do the *zouk* together. . .'

'Better not,' says Delia, and laughs.

*

'My brother thought you were a special case,' says his sister, the Be-Linda, Linda. 'Farouche – that was his word.'

'Can you make someone else out of me?' asks Masha, curious.

'I can make you look tasty, but maybe no one puts you in their mouth,' says Linda. 'Can you walk a tightrope? That way you must look up. Politics?'

'Oh no,' says Masha. 'I can't sit still.'

'I mean the real thing, Masha. Food and guns, not sitting – though I can sit for hours. I wear these clothes – pink and blue. Like hydrangeas – you need to drink a lot,' says Linda.

'Batik,' says Masha, fingering. 'It's been out for fifty years. But you're nude beneath.'

'That way you're poor and hunted. No drawers, no heels,' says Linda. 'It helps you get a better deal, makes you sharpen up. Your skin, so intricate and improvised, your *mappa mundi* – you feel it sitting there beside, beneath you, hiding your face, itching and cooling, sweating, spiced and billowing. . . Curious infestations, tracks of missing galleons, new continents on horizons never spied, lilting to moons and stars that pinch and pull. . . I dress old, Masha, but unlike you, not ancient. Age brings not wisdom, but a sag. It says, "don't touch – or I might breach". Authority and preciousness, my dear.'

'Well, Linda,' Masha says, not much impressed. 'I'm in a bag of skin as well. What can you do for me?'

'You've had enough world, Masha,' Linda says. 'But you can't get out. Imagine – those rockets – space. You don't just step in and turn the key. It's worse than firing squads – the nausea, the interviews, the baggy suit. Then you must come back, and they don't believe you went. Besides – there's bugger all up there that hasn't been tonsured, watered, hoed, down here. We've gardeners, good as any in the galaxy. We've acid lakes and burning bush, blizzards of plastic corks – just like on Mars. No. I won't withdraw. I'll go up high, and run it all. They're my court, poor dears: politicos – on the stump and caricatured. The actresses – stripping off, pretending to get fucked. Philosophers with their views on dogfood and on motor cars. . . In the stocks and in the public view. I see them all – they're pawns, dear Masha, poor feeble things! I'm king and queen – for ever: there's no one plays with me. Beyond defeat and victory, that's where you must be – a set of reds, a court, imperial pieces all lined up, victorious: no contest, no opposition.'

'You could be the whites,' says Masha, impressed.

'The whites are scum,' says Linda. 'The reds, the blacks – they're all the same: you must be menacing, is all. Where you come from, Masha dear – the Mongols mangled it! Humiliated the Russians, then in came the Brits, the French, the Yankees, doodling on the maps. . . It was so good before all that: the contests between the blues and greens! Afterwards – empires and persecution, countries and chaos.'

'Yes,' Masha says, 'that sounds quite right. But it's irrelevant. Take me up with you, we'll have our roost and watch the chickens scratch below. . .'

'Hold on,' says Linda. 'That'd be the easy way for you. I can't adopt you, Masha. You're not a sister, nor a daughter. You're a supplicant, so you must bend and fawn.'

'No,' says Masha. 'No games.'

'You haven't understood,' says Linda. 'I don't bet. You're not my clown. I have you do what you can do – that's all, it's more than people usually get.'

'What am I, Linda?' Masha asks. 'What do I want?'

'You're spoiled, Masha,' Linda says. 'You've been dropped and trampled. Parts are missing.'

'All right,' says Masha. 'I can go with that. I'll let you put me where I want to go.'

'That's about right,' says Linda. 'Be loyal!'

*

'I could become like you, Linda,' says Masha.

'I'm a dried out gourd,' says Linda. 'Don't think it. Don't join. It's nothing, vain. I could paint you up, make you play the suffering of the world. Nothing, Masha, it's all nothing and the powers that take you up – they're nothing too. Avoid me. Get in that rocket, circle the earth. Come down silent in the desert, not a word, and start again. Don't try to do anything new. Nor old. Just walk, drink that orange water from the pond, that tastes of copper. Hope you don't see anyone, no one at all, not the wolfman, not the man with the tarry sack, not the woman with the axle pin. No one. And die. Go into dust, be clean once and for all.'

'Yes,' says Masha. 'I think that's what I want.'

*

This place – she escaped here. They didn't want her, but her story's on her voice – a refugee.

There's processions here – you walk along, no need to believe in anything – the martyred ancestor, carried along, you can flagellate, and no one minds. There's fire-walking – a secret.

*

'Tell me, Delia,' Masha asks, 'do they do exorcisms here?'

'Oh yes,' says Delia, 'the service is complete, from conception right to paradise.'

'I don't know if I want the devil out, or more put in,' says Masha. 'It seems you can't do it for yourself. A pity you're so flighty, Delia, or you could help, and pull it out, like delivering a calf, or push it in, like frog legs being swallowed. . .'

'You'll do well, Masha,' Delia says, intimidated. 'You're so commanding.'

'Well,' says Masha, 'my little handicap. . . I can't climb up the rope.'

'Don't let her up,' shouts Alina, but the rope is knotted, up you go, like a staircase. . . It's hot, summer's end, goodbye. . .

'Goodbye, Mother,' Masha remembers the poem. 'Standing at the window, Transparent as a cocoon. . . Don't be a bitch, Alina – everyone has mothers.'

'Oh, you're up, Masha,' says Alina. 'Don't rock us. Drink from the bottle, there's no glass.'

'The seer has a glass eye – he looks through the stone with it,' says Delia, making conversation. 'Then they burned him in a tar-barrel on the beach. Best focus on what's before you!'

'Drink, Masha,' Alina says. 'Imagine you're nearly there, the waves are flat – don't rock the tree, the boat, there's no one on the beach, no seer, no lookout. . .'

'Look out!' shouts Delia – but the rocking's now extreme: Alina falls.

'That's tragic!' Masha says. 'I had a hiatus – not knowing what ought to come next – dogs have that confusion – there's instinct, and there's context. Double perspective. Uncertainty – barking when they want to bite. . .'

'Yes, what can we do next?' Delia asks, confused. 'There were too many of us up there – but . . . lightening the load, they tell you to . . . and now, my sister: if she isn't dead, she'll for sure be paralysed.'

'Lay her here, quiet, in the bushes,' Masha says as the two survivors skitter down the rope.

'Murderers,' says Alina weakly. 'Fuck you. I know your intentions. . .'

'But, Alina dear,' says Delia, 'I had none. Maybe Masha. . .? People do want me for myself, you know, to be alone with me. . .'

'I'm sure it isn't that,' Alina says. 'It could have been the breeze. We're all quite drunk besides – maybe that's why I can't stand or feel my legs.'

'It's a puzzle,' Masha says. 'Are you sure it's digging in my intentions that's the best next step? If I cure you, Alina, maybe it'll be passed on to me, your weakness. And – yes, I'm bound to Delia – not sex, absolutely.'

'She's very quiet,' says Delia. 'Propped there in that bush.'

'She'll be fine,' says Masha. 'She's much stronger than us.'

They stare at Alina's face, it's a white cheese floating in a bowl, a blancmange, curds and whey, they think. Alina thinks she's going somewhere. 'Help me!' she says, but doesn't need it.

'Look!' shouts Masha. 'The tree – it's calm.'

There wasn't room up there – Delia, Alina – they were used to it, it was their fairy-tale, a tiny platform, up among the apes and parrots – if you had a basket you could stay for ever, not doing good, and nothing bad you could have done.

'There's a problem, Masha,' Delia says. 'The basket. Alina filled it. Now. . .'

'You go back to Doctor Gritt,' says Masha. 'Then you can fill the basket. Society's like that – you each depend. There's icon painters, filling shotgun cartridges, and keeping wills, and boiling tar: a place for all, quite automatically. Communities are better still. . . It's like diluted family, and all go daily to the mosque, the church, or round the stones . . . all together, and embrace.'

'I don't fancy it, Masha,' Delia says. 'Listen – we're doing experiments. Do you believe in the immortal soul?'

'I'd need to think,' says Masha.

'Gritt says we'd run a current through the faith-filled volunteer. You, Masha, you could be the chosen one. You'd be the conductor, for ever a live wire – there'd be eternity in every wall, behind the switch. . .' says Delia.

'I've thought, Delia,' Masha says, 'and no, I don't believe about the souls. Besides – if there's transmigration, some bodies, crawling, living underneath the tiles – they'd be too small to rig and plug. . .'

'Keep it in mind,' says Delia. 'Things are changing. Fear, hope, vendetta. People want to come together – fascism, Masha. Architecture with huge spaces, columns tall to match. It gives a frisson, like strangers' legs that touch beneath the cafe table. . .'

'It won't hit me,' says Masha. 'I'm a chameleon, I can paint my face, if that's the thing. The tree – the family tree? We're underneath it, Delia – it's solid, but it bends beneath the breeze. Doctor Gritt – oh, he'll join anything. Call it fascism, or any kind of strife; genetic bent. I've lived there, so has he. If you can't fight, you run. For you, Delia, it'll be a novelty. Electricity – that's not political: that's your thing. Just pretend to be enthused when there is nothing you can celebrate.'

They look up, through the leaves – maybe the clouds will give a sign? But no, they fleet away, and change their shapes.

'Alina! Oh no! I should react – there's nothing in the books – it's always someone "like". . . Missed "like" a brother or a sister, never the real thing. You've had sisters too, Masha, lost them. What does one do?' asks Delia.

'It has to be unique, and personal,' says Masha. 'The grief. Think – the wind . . . blew her away, the cresting waves turned her to green and blue, off she went, over the horizons . . . like a sailfish in the deep. . .'

'Oh yes,' says Delia, 'that's beautiful. Beauty – it resolves all things. It's mystic, but it lies outside front doors, there – the lilac bush, syringa – reminding you of nymphs. . . Oh dear – it all seems bushes . . . that's where Alina ends. . . Perhaps she kept a diary? We could peek and publish, maybe empathise. . .'

Nothing's resolved. The basket question . . . the questioning hook hangs on its rope.

'Most places,' Masha says, 'have lists of people to be persecuted – too feisty or too quiet, too passive or too organised. Alina was lucky – she left before the overture. Everything was fortuitous – if she'd clung to her branch, she'd be up there still, and we'd have tipped instead.'

'I often wonder,' Delia says, after her silent tears, 'if we are buffaloes. Males solitary, females all clumped under a matriarchal gendarmerie. . .'

'Oh Delia,' Masha says, 'you're much too young to think of buffaloes. If I'd not been ravaged so, and had my mind disturbed by complex thoughts that I'd not tell to you, nor even on TV – I'd go back, join Doctor Gritt again, and help him save the world, a device like all those other turnarounds – morse code, canned food. . .'

'I feel that's where I too should be,' says Delia. 'In the tree – we shan't grow wings and feed on grubs. I'm young it's true – but ever day I grow a little closer, Masha, to you and all your tragedies. Childhood and innocence – where'd they go?'

'Not to remember shows you had them,' Masha says.

'The birds have eaten all the mulberries. Our time is up.'

*

There's a long wait to see this guy – most places, he wouldn't be employed, nor would his work exist. He says to Masha, 'See – your mates have saved the world, and you ducked out. You can't be helped. . . ' His job – is help.

'It's done,' says Masha, 'It'll last a while – that thing, invention, that's to last for ever. I did my bit.'

'I'm sure you'll find your happiness,' the guy says, thinking of his own, starting his own tear of hope.

Masha looks down her tunnel – men, women, waiting, mostly poor, a small room that smells of what's gone on elsewhere. The future – no mystery.

That's pretty good. Worth an apostasy, for sure.

*

'Masha – how I miss her,' Delia says. 'She was like a sister. More sisterly than my sister. There was a storm, we all fell – our parents too, distant relatives more distant still – many of our memories can't ever be recovered. All fell off the tree, and many disappeared for good. Or bad.

I'm leaving for Brazil. I'm one of those who saved the world, you know, I'm owed a trip.'

The guy, her team-mate Furio, asks, 'And Masha?'

'Oh, she'll be somewhere,' Delia says. 'She always managed better far than me.'

'Another country? On the world's underside? The idea's frightening,' Furio says, kidding her along.

'Oh, I'm not at all the domestic type,' says Delia. 'I want the colours round me, the beautiful tints – the people, that is. Cinnamon, biscuit . . . and in every room, the parrots. . .'

'There's snakes like rubber pipelines,' Furio says.

'It's the song,' says Delia, '"Take it easy, my brother Charlie": I thought how a brother could be like a sister too, with some accessories. I'd fly. There's all the cash we'll get from Doctor Gritt's invention that we made. Think of those trees, the big steaks, the happy hours with yellow drinks. . .'

'Don't be disappointed, Delia,' says Furio. 'Brothers and sisters are like parents, they just come along. It's not like swans and parrots, imprisoned in the egg and pecking out, staying together ever after.'

'I'm a happy one,' says Delia. '"All men are brothers", they say: so, "all women must be sisters"!'

'That's what they used to say,' says Furio. 'It's not

like that. I went for sex to Rio – all I got was smiles. And spits. The secret of cohabitation, Delia – there was your tree . . . the silken clothes you were to weave. . .'

'Oh yes,' says Delia. 'We weren't competitive. Masha – maybe too much. So – poor Alina. The birds ate all the worms before us. But – science drives me, Furio. In Brazil – there is a settlement. They call it "Uncle Charlie". All the tribes – they've gone corrupt. This group, they start right from the beginning, though you can keep your pants on, no poison arrows, no grinding porridge on your thighs. We brainy guys – we do the history of the world, in presto time. It's science, Furio – what we get, we write it up, and if we don't survive, the last one leaves a pic.'

'Doctor Gritt took all our cash,' says Furio. 'Invested it. A blackjack system – if he wins . . . we can go anywhere, all of us. If you're lost, Delia, I'll find a way to bring you . . . where you want to be.'

'I'll go anywhere to do research,' says Delia. 'And you, Furio?'

'Dogs look for dogs. I look for people,' Furio says. 'It's what we do. There's nothing else.'

*

'Just call me Ben,' says Father Ben. 'Welcome, Delia: our tribe's not born from women, nor from eggs. It's planes that bring you ready grown, more or less ready for the flight. . .'

'One thing,' says Delia. 'The basket. How's it filled? I've lived on those bounds between nurture and the rest. Nature betrayed us. My mother didn't nurture long enough. We fell out the nest.'

'Oh,' says Ben, fingering his body paint. 'We're not a commune. We don't hunt. Nor sell our trees and sit out on the porch. I do some trade with happiness, forgetfulness as well. It does not impinge on us, dear Delia. All will be clear, if you're inquisitive enough.'

'Too bad,' says Delia. 'I'm no good at selling, even happiness – I hear trading drugs is dangerous, too. I saw myself more along with parrots, picking the fruit for them. . .'

'Oh Delia,' says Ben, and laughs, 'Not that sort of drug! – I sell cures. You forget you're sick and so you're happy! It's being good! How could you think. . . ?'

'It all seems much the same,' says Delia. 'My sister Masha started off a surgeon, then the ethic tripped her up. . .'

'We hoped Masha would have come,' says Ben. 'Our parabola – follows the dips and spurts of many nations' destinies. Take China – how the empire's history wavered . . . then it all came back, better, stronger. . . First the disaster, then the winning streak.'

'You mean the Mongols?' Delia says. 'That wasn't Masha, I am sure. Chinese history's a lesson to us all, but she's been elsewhere. . .'

'History's the only lesson, Delia,' says Ben. 'It doesn't matter where you start. Remember – it doesn't teach a thing. Cling close to that. It's the most important part. . . The place, the time – doesn't have the slightest influence.'

'You mean it does have influence, but you're not bothered?' Delia asks.

'Well, Delia,' says Ben, 'that all comes to the same, I think.'

'I want to meet the others,' Delia says.

'See, Delia,' Ben says, hitching up his undershorts, 'most settlements like ours – they want to do it all at once, and end in profit. They start from the happy end. Time's short, they say. The space ship's on its way. The crops are ripe, the dope's run out, the sages' pot of ink ran dry, the guru's spent the cash . . . the guys aren't happy and the gals have run away. . . You must have read it all. None of those experiments ends well, although they wanted to fulfil the prophecy in marching time. . . It doesn't work. You have to undergo it like the Chinese do . . . the warring states, the nomads, horses, disaster – the exam rooms closed, the scrolls tossed in the well – and then recovery, a purging – and you're off again. Sail round the world, or lock the doors, smoke your smoke or join the boxing club – you see, Delia, that's why we wanted Masha here. . . She had that kernel of experience . . . she'd lived it all: collapse, her principle proclaimed, a life regretted nonetheless, escapes and hardships. . .'

'I see all that,' says Delia. 'I told you: more than a sister. Now, where is all the rest?'

'Oh, I'm the king they chased away, plague-ridden, the loser, the old schlock. . .' says Ben, sobbing. 'It's most fortuitous. I'm on my own. I shall be back. I'll choose the whitest horse. Maybe I'll string the traitors up – maybe an educative camp. . .'

'I can't wait here for centuries,' Delia says. 'Let me see my sisters in the trees – for sure, they'll ask you back.'

'No, Delia, you haven't understood,' says Ben. 'You think that everything is for the best, that I am good, and that it all ends well. It isn't so. We are–' and he laughs '–*in medias res*: stuck in the midst.'

'I could go home,' says Delia, starting to cry, thinking of Alina, someone to hide behind . . . no one, nothing. . .

'You haven't got the fare,' says Ben.

'There's Furio,' Delia thinks. 'But he knows it's not at all like I had thought . . . though it's identical to what he thought. . . What would he do, what would I do. . . ?'

'Ben, you must be one of the rare good ones,' Delia says. 'It's always so – the old blind king is chased away, kisses the witch, returns as a youth with flaxen hair. . . Tell me, at least, that you were good.'

'No, not at all,' says Ben, quite angry. 'I was like brother Charlie – took it easy. All of it, the stock and pot I took. . . The trouble is – after the king's dethroned, there come the emperors. . . Once more I'm short, dear Delia, of some cash. . . '

'Oh no,' she says, 'even my panties are borrowed ones. I came ready for democracy, the tribe around the fire . . . symposia. . . '

'That wasn't it at all,' says Ben.

He's gross, a bear, massive, magnificent. Wicked. He weeps again. 'I have this *time* to live,' he says. 'To live right through each second, and for what?'

'I know,' says Delia, touched by his ignorance. 'This country, where I never was before – it was a pile of countries, each with a magic. Not now. It's all one, the big and little people with their sports. "A day in itself exists and the one before exists, and the one before the one before . . . and you never get to live *yourself,* but only to live *life.*" That's what you mean?'

'And suppose it was for me, the time lived, all mine,' he says. 'What would it be for? For me? For itself – time lived to show it's time, and nothing more?'

'Well, Ben,' Delia says, 'there's been a lot of that sort – of time like a forest, and men who didn't know that there were other men, and regretted it when they found out. . .'

'As you know, Delia,' says Ben, brightening up, 'there were parrots in those trees – all sorts, and colours you'd go crazy looking in your paintbox for.'

In this clearing, there is yellow mud – you could shape a bird from it, and in this heat you could bake it hard, blow into it and make it sing. Then, Brother Ben does things no brother ought to do, and Delia thinks it would be better to have gone straight up to the sky, and not have had the extra burden of a death. Ben is being the king estranged, despised – and it is right it should be so, and Delia wants him transfixed by a thousand bamboo sticks, and somewhere in the forest are her hungry sisters wishing they could find the fruit and eat it quick, that takes them straight to paradise and leave their lumpish bodies in a heap or, better, in the quicksand, and when it's day it's night to come and so and so.

'It was my mistake, I'm finished here,' says Delia. 'It should have been . . . science, living for ever. Instead of songs – forging another kind of truth. Who'd want what I've run into. . . ?'

*

Among the trees, there's people, huddled. 'Where's your clothes?' Regina asks.

'Oh,' Delia says. 'Who cares about my suitcase? There was this guy – king of China, then there's war, an emperor, more war – democracy . . . No doubt that he's a genius . . . Ben, the impaler. He told the past, the future – and he hurts. Himself – and me.'

'What China?' asks Regina. 'I thought it was America. Yes – he's a genius. He's the disenchanter. Joining a settlement to end in goodness! – it's right that you replay the past, go onwards with its burden, not learning, just supporting. Here, it's called the undulating snake. America – they were always keen on slaves. There was the mad king over the seas, lots of slaves, a war, and then an empire, more slaves, war everywhere. That's what we were, we are – the slaves. We ran – into the forest, with the animals. That is civilisation.'

'I'm not into all that,' says Delia. 'We made Doctor

Gritt's new gewgaw that would guarantee our lives for ever – energy that's not dispersed, it lasts. . .'

'My dear!' Regina says. 'That was naive. Did you think? When you made it and weren't paid? Did you imagine Ben, and us? Your master must have been Pangloss – and here you are, Candide set loose to wander, your round eyes looking for a crust of someone else's pizza. . . That Ben – he's always in character: you have to run! That's all.'

'I'm not naive,' says Delia, 'just naked. . . '

'Here!' Regina says, 'you are our spirit, come from the forest, a sacrifice escaping embers or the knife. . .'

Her sisters bring a cloak, a hat. 'It's wonderful. . .' says Delia, calming down. 'But – the feathers – not parrots'? Spare me that!'

'It's true,' Regina says. 'We slaves – we're only coloured cinnamon and biscuit. Ben said we needed brightening up. Your cloak – the feathers aren't just parrots', there is perroquets' and papagayos' too. There's every colour in the world, and through the leaves comes every light that changes them to every colour in the galaxy. . .'

'It's not like that,' says Delia, weeping for the birds, 'Colour and light are indissoluble, it's all to do with frequency . . . .'

‘Of course,’ Regina says, ‘these birds are not so frequent now. It’s yours, my dear, their heritage. You must respect them, but – don’t wear it into town, that cloak, and now this hat, this crown . . . You can pretend the mad king had a queen, dressed to fly away.’

And she puts a crimson hat on Delia . . .

‘Stand over there,’ Regina says. ‘Don’t speak, hold out your hand. If there’s insults, don’t react. There’s foreign guys – they’ve come to see the football match. If you get foreign change – you can buy clothes.’

Delia begs well. ‘It’s all coin, mostly Thai,’ she tells Regina. ‘It can’t be changed.’

‘Cash – capital – and telephones – it keeps us all together, makes the world tiny, but still round, they say,’ Regina tells her. ‘We can’t help you, though. We’ve none of what it takes: no capital, no telephones. Some want to leave, but don’t know where. Some want to stay, but don’t know what they’d do if.’

An old, old man throws weeds and stuff down from his balcony. ‘If I make a pipe,’ says Delia, ‘this could be reed. . . And study hard, making some tunes, maybe I could buy a telephone.’

‘We’re all in conflict, Delia,’ says Regina. ‘Something could come of that. Severe analysis, all ours, with no intermediaries, no professionals. Important for the species, too. We can't be bothered with your underwear.'

'If I were a virtuoso on this pipe, studying all day and some nights too – I'd earn and use the telephone to call to Furio, and leave,' says Delia.

'If you learned well, you wouldn't need to leave. But – that's a crap instrument,' Regina says. 'And you've no ear. You'd need a bundle of them strapped alongside, like in Peru, and a choir of you and mates: you'd also need the clothes they wear, a different hat as well.'

'I can't stay here,' says Delia, 'and nor can you, it seems, Regina.'

'I can do anything,' Regina says. 'It's that these systems that we have to live by, whatever place you are – they keep on hitting the back wall. They can't go forward. They can't survive. Yet they survive: – there comes a wriggle, a man of destiny, something borrowed, stolen – sometimes though, the balance is lost for good. But usually . . . it rears again on its hind legs. That's evolution! Does it damage us, we who're here, observing, as goats and guinea pigs, these cataclysms, the demagicking that leaves you in the mud? Of course it does! We're here to damage and be damaged. It's of no consequence. No one wrings their hands for us. Go ahead, Delia – wring yours for yourself. Don't think that blowing that goddam pipe will get you out. . .'

'The old, old guy – he tries to help, I think,' says Delia. 'Though maybe not. And, Regina: systems breaking down . . . you guys make your own dilemma, add it to everybody else's.'

'You've been asleep for centuries, Delia,' Regina says, irritated. 'It's the way it is. We're up against the back wall too. Our bodies are long obsolete, our grey brains have some help from electricians, but we go deeper, deeper in our hole we've dug – our spades are long a mile, the rocky soil grows ever hotter, liquid anthracite. . . Talk to Semyon. He'll tell you what's collapsing, what can't be shored up, how fast it happens, whether to run or face it out.'

'It's like that horse in Dostoevsky,' Delia says. 'It's beaten and it falls. Then it gets up.'

'I think it didn't,' says Regina. 'Besides, it's all a metaphor. The driver beats himself, beats us. We're him. His anger's masochistic, he destroys his livelihood. Down to the bottom, where there's no one to exploit, you've only destitution, suffering. Your dead horse . . .'

'I know all that,' says Delia. 'Most people run to where there's plenty. They don't wait for paradise and death – they go where things are working fine. . .'

'That's the point we're at,' Regina says. 'Our dilemma. You don't add anything.'

'You're all foreigners,' says Delia. 'What if we had a past? Here? Let's try gene sequences upon my flute, and that way change our essences. Some gentle engineering. . . New bodies, larger heads, more beautiful the faces, smooth and smiley, and brainier the brains. . . Or I could improvise on time – maybe get it running backwards, so we have a longer stretch before?'

The old, old man hears everything: 'Go to!' he shouts. 'Set my clock to run in counter-time, put quarter-tones into those scales – let's escape dodecaphony, on with the microtones! Alas! our undiscerning ears – attuned to danger whistles, the sirens on the ambulance and the morning cock! And yet – the path is there. Start again: into the forest, off with your clothes – communicate with clicks and grins, your rituals lasting seven years, you come of age at eighty-five. . . Do everything different, more ghastly, more refined. You're born to be sectarians, you, Regina, all your mates . . . here is your birthing room . . . "escape"'s the first word you will speak. . . '

'This reed,' asks Delia, busking. 'Its music's not too fluid? Ending in Hawaian glides?'

'You may be right,' the old man says. 'No songs, then, and no piping. That Pan was no musician – the gigs were just to gather groupies. Yet – if only He had held his course – we need a superpower like Him. Direct, no electronics, and no capital. All see and do.'

'Show me around,' says Delia. 'Show me the country. My sisters, brothers, even if they're not related.'

The old man walks round, very, very slow. So slow, the stand of trees seems more extensive than it is. There's a few tall trunks. A few skewed huts, an angry voice, nasal and insistent. A long nose that – a tapir's.

'It's much, much smaller than I'd thought, the place. . .' says Delia.

The old man doesn't answer, looks expectant. Not his fault the place is large or small. It's a classic – you need to know the place of the observer, the uniqueness or not of the phenomenon, the scale . . . It's physics. Those requirements – you must establish them – being smaller than you think: it's true, it isn't scientific, Delia thinks. It's almost a self-criticism.

'Is there any more?' she asks the old, old man.

'Obviously, there's all inside the huts, inside the people, on the branches, in the bark. I'm going to lie down,' he says.

*

It must be Semyon, the analyst, his the tapir's nose, the long argument. 'Go, or stay. This capitalism – or that?

Will it end good, just go on?'

Semyon says to Delia, 'We didn't come here to make previsions, but to keep in step. When we've done the past – we speed up into what comes next, through, and out the other side.'

'The old, old man,' says Delia. 'He's so old he could be immortal.'

'That doesn't follow,' Semyon says. 'But, yes, he might be. Do we wait and see? No, it's not about the individual. He's a survival from the last experiment. The only one. Does that mean it was successful? And if he lives for ever?'

'I don't see the point,' says Delia. 'You're speeding up our social life. Why not relax and wait and see? You guys, my sisters too – you want to see if there'll be war between you. Or if there's a way to stop the cart that's racing down the slope. . .'

'The problem is,' Regina says, taking over, 'the horse is dead. Who's next to go between the shafts?'

'Maybe this Delia would do,' says Semyon, not kindly. 'What do you do, Delia? Can you be a brake?'

'I'm an eclectic engineer,' says Delia. 'If you say "electrical" they want you to fix the light. We – or Doctor Gritt – made energy saved to last for ever . . . or as long as we could stand to watch.'

'Oh yes?' asks Semyon. 'Longer than the sun? The galaxy?'

'We didn't ask. We split up when we had to socialise. My sister Masha. . .' Delia thinks of nurturing trees, Alina, and she starts to cry. 'Show me my sisters, Semyon,' she says. 'I'm a refugee, from paradise, and now you analytical guys, obsidian hard. . . Here, you have space – instead of you sectarian ones jousting and being rough – why don't you fill this continent, this emporium, compendium, this all of everything – with people looking for a home. . .?'

'What!' Regina shouts. 'Expropriate the Indians, cut down the parrots' trees. . . ?'

'There's only that old man, his balcony gone arid – he forgot to water, there's just stalks and fuzz. . .' says Semyon. 'It's a possibility – yes. We can wait to see if the old guy really is immortal. What then, what if he is – and we are not? Is not – we are? No, Regina, we have the choice: fight it out. Not as humanitarians, but as comrades who want to run the show, and stay in place. Let the defeated leave, if that is what they must. The other possibility – is that those leave, who can't defend themselves, or can't see places for them when they lose.'

'No, Semyon,' Regina shouts. 'There may be war – the system's fallen down. There may be peace – just the same, the system's fallen down. Or partly falls. . . In mid air – maybe that's not scientific, the middle air – you mightn't understand. . .'

'For reason,' Delia interrupts. 'All this is guessing. Delusion, wishful thought or hope, or moral certainty. What strikes me – and I'm the engineer – is that the old, old guy threw down the reed, the length of straw. That's what the music bigwig did – the god. He's certain of his immortality. . .'

'Oh no!' says Semyon. 'He cleaned his mess – no one was transmogrified, no magic biscuit or a glass of mescal, no trick, no truck, no hidden string, no panels, no connivance – no! No intimation of his immortality. A dirty guy that cleans his house.'

'Who does indeed have intimations!' Delia says. 'Throwing down a pipe, like Pan. . .'

'Maybe that's what he thinks,' says Regina. 'He's lived long because he's a brother Charlie, taking it easy.'

'Cure me!' the old, old man, for sure a brother Charlie, shouts. 'I'm stiff all over, my bones are rotting – you, with the shaman's cape, Delia – cure me!'

'I don't know medicine,' says Delia. 'Energy – that's immortal. Yours is running out. I can't do anything. Eat well, eat natural – monkeys, lizards – those big inquisitive ants. That is the best – I can't be of more use .

. . I can't even play your flute. . .'

'Maybe you should take your tibia,' says this brother Charlie, 'out of your leg, like in the picture books, suck out the marrow, drill the holes – and blow. Otherwise – your feathered cape – just covers a wretched skeleton. . .'

'Yes!' Delia shouts up. 'That is precisely so. I'm emptied out. Ben – he did it. Emptied me! They chased him out – but he's the persuasive kind – all the expelled kings are full of blarney juice, waiting to be asked back, looking for some vacancy. People should be severe. The guillotine! That's the historic way.'

'Stop shouting, Delia,' Regina shouts. 'It's not your fight. We're foreigners, but you're more foreign still. Forget the history – that greedy bag of bones, uninvited slurper, crashing every feast. Have done too with that old, old man – obsessive tidier, the best thing he threw out with all that garden waste, was music. . . He's a perfectionist, and those unpredicted sounds got on his nerves. . .'

'It's true,' says Delia. 'And yet, this instrument – it doesn't work. I'll not self-mutilate, cut off my leg to make a better tune – I'm not as bold as Masha, the only true and loving sister I have left. She's a survivor – I am not. She went back, into the primitive – the flight, the torture, storm at sea, the hunt – all that. If I can't play my flute, I'll hang it in a tree and let the air do what it wills. I'll find some wire and make an organ, one with stops for every sound that's in the earth and in the sea – then drive it, like a cart, sitting there, it rises up, billowing, and sinks in pink and purple lovelights. . .'

She rambles on, and from the sisters' hut, she hears the voices – terrible and menacing, 'No, no – the contradiction isn't here – not in Brazil. No one would want another dose of prisons and electroshocks. . .'

'Maybe not for themselves, but for the others. . .' comes another voice.

'We're sisters, honouring the decencies – dissenters – they should be put out, civilly, into the other hut, the brothers' thorny nest. . .'

'The contradiction lies at sea – the other side – Americans against Chinese, that's what they want, two spavined naked wrestlers on a threadbare mat. . .'

'That pope gave the Atlantic to Brazil, the trees galore, the golden men, the silver maidens, he gave up his God – the gods who came here, they were from Benin and Senegal. . . '

'It's obsolete, all this,' Regina interjects, raging through the door. 'Let's go back to our original debate – there, we're on surer ground. I say – non-figurative painting's painting of the void. It's our absence, abdication. The world we lose when we have gone. It's like equations. . .'

'Reactionary thoughts – belong in the brothers' hut,' says a commanding voice. 'If it's equations you invoke – those reach for perfection, symmetry. And if there is no naked legs and breasts – so be it! Let it be so. That wasn't our reality – just myth! And remember, no comments on our bodies, please!'

'You cover everything,' says Delia, admiring, as Regina joins her, seeming flustered and put out, 'Aesthetics, minorities – nationalism, linguistics too. . .'

'Yes, we're well-rounded, Delia: and – my body is the best. It needs no commentary – I can be virgin, mother, model, victim – none of that rubs off on my inside. . .'

Semyon comes from the sisters' hut: 'Everyone is split,' he says with pride. 'The brothers – armed struggle or the football. The sisters – stay or go. My work is done. The contradictions are laid bare – things will get better, even worse . . . I'm off. They often bring the old king back, forget the bullying. . .'

'We too may be on our way,' says Regina, grabbing Delia's arm, rolling her eyes at the colours of the cloak, colours of everything, with nothing of itself, a *mémoire* of skinned parrots.

'Tell me dear,' Regina says to Delia, and wriggles at

her with a thin mauve tongue, 'give me a sip, my love – your nectar. . .'

'I'm not sure. . .' says Delia, pulling away.

'Your chubby face, those curls, the off-white sheep, tumbling down around your throat. . .' says Regina. 'The energy. Where d'you get it? Do you suck on wires, or can your tongue fit inside the walls and draw it out? We've a long journey, a thousand steps at least. . . The vital juice. . . I need to drink it down, your youth, your current, a deep draught.'

They move towards the highway. They chat, they wheedle. Do people here stop? Who do they resemble, those three hitchers – a menace? An epiphany? – a queen, a knave, a rainbow bird? A winning hand – but for which game?

From the huts, there's angry shouting. Gunfire, or sticks.

'I should have been a Trot,' says Semyon. 'A rich Trot. I sure know how to split.'

'Oh my poor sisters,' Regina keens. 'And all those brothers who I never saw,' says Delia.

There's nothing to be done. The fight goes on. 'Maybe the police. . .'

'No, no,' says Semyon. 'That would finish everyone.'

'Why don't those who want to stay, just stay: and

leave – they leave.'

'Delia!' Regina says. 'Our is an experiment. It's to be followed to the end. Besides – there are the huts – those cost. Principles and lovers, cash in the mattress. All that, and more. We came here to see how it would work out, life on earth – listen! I wonder where they got the guns?'

'That's not so hard,' says Semyon, pushing the other two along the road. 'It's important to see who will survive. Without some winners – there's no test.'

'But Semyon,' says Delia. 'One thing's what happens in a country, a continent – those were just scientists in a spat. . .'

'Don't underestimate,' says Semyon. 'That is the point – to see why one does one thing, and one another. That's what fascinates. What else is there? What else is to know?'

'Oh, energy,' says Delia. 'I know all about that and it's quite different from people – it is one thing. But that's not the end of it.'

'You're telling me!' says Semyon, laughing. 'I was an altar boy. I *am* an altar boy. With all the perversions! The whip. Like in Dosteovsky.'

'The horse? The peasant?' Delia asks, and laughs, perturbed by all the violent deaths, down in the clearing, pursuers flicking through the trees.

'I think you know, sweet Delia,' says Semyon, sliding his hand beneath her feathers. 'How it ends.'

Delia pulls away. 'You remember – the soul, liberated, flies back to the bough, the tree of life,' she says.

Regina pulls a face, displeased. Delia thinks of Masha, her disfigured hand, the turmoil flattening out – a calm that lasts and lasts, like a flat beach, a flat umber, acrylic. . .

Delia laughs. 'A hand disfigured? How stupid! What a thought – the figure is the face, of course. Masha, my sister. Her face was beautiful, or so I think – behind the veil.'

'They are all beautiful, behind the veil,' Regina says. 'Just as all souls have all the colours of the parrot – how they squawk! The sound gets lost, of course – a highway, trafficked like this one, where no one stops, mutes everything.'

'They're afraid of us,' says Delia, 'No one will stop. And – Semyon – now I remember – not a whip. It was a four-by-four. You can't kill something with a whip.'

'There's a lot of energy in a whip,' Regina says. 'You'd need every bit of energy to do a standing jump, into the tree. . .'

'Oh, that's what they thought you could,' says Delia.

'The soul was energy, immortal. That's what it meant – flighty like a bird. Strong enough to shake the tree. If you weren't holding on as hard as possible. . . You were in luck, Regina – you were uncertain – leave and live, or stay and maybe you would need to fight, or be a victim, hero or martyr both and – here you are! you didn't have to choose – that's what you can hope for – walking away, not deciding.'

'Oh, I'd decided,' Regina says, as they walk along the road.

*

A pickup passes them, veering on the shoulder to make dust on them – in the back is Ben, he swoops off Delia's queenly hat and squawks, hunching up and down.

'Take it easy, brother Charlie!' the three hikers shout, making the gesture.

'He'll be waiting for us when we get there,' Semyon says.

*

'There, you didn't suffer,' Semyon says, when they get there, where they didn't want to go.

'Even a little is enough,' Regina says.

'That's the flaw in humanism,' Delia says. 'Practise. You get used to it, seeing those things in cages, as a scientist. Suffering saves the world.' She thinks – Alina suffered hardly anything. That's why the world's no nearer being saved. Masha made the sacrifice – maybe she's making out with Furio – that'd be another one, each whipping on the other, no Masha's finger to point them on,to wherever they don't want to go.

*

'You get a white coat,' says the captain, 'so's you blend. It's white on white, iced in. There's rounds of ice, a slender green, like you find on dead men's fingernails. From our tall ship – it's prawn crackers, gone soggy, far as you can't see. . . There's fun below – there's dancing rites when crewmen spot a living thing, or if one's blown over, becomes a marble block, more beautiful than Phidias made, there's arms down by his sides – the breasts imaginary – but then, my dear, sex without love is second always to love without sex. . . You'd better join the dance – or else it's you, iced out. We pretend, of

course, we're warm and valuable – but the sky! the winds that scour, the air like gypsum clouds – it's like you find on Jupiter, the seas like what they had on Mars until they blew themselves to powdered deserts, just like we are dallying with . . . . There's entertainment – jug and bones a speciality, movies – we have what we've found in cairns – there's all the Lassies, Doktor Mabuse, The Murderers Among Us – we know them all by heart. You'll find,' and he strips off Delia's cloak of many parrots, gives her the scientific robe, 'the white gives a prevision of the time you are all bone – nothing will eat your flesh, you'll dry out like a cod, and wisps of you will blow and frolic down the centuries. . .'

'This white coat,' Delia says. 'Has a black streak down the back.'

'That's so we see you if we dump you on the ice, if you don't join in the rites, or you get sick or mutinous – you'll be inquisitive, and desperate – and with the stripe, you'll look quite penguin-like. Adele penguins – they would love to hitch with us, like you – but we don't stop; a moment – and you're blocked for ever, our red and green ship just a stain, a flash, a blink – in seconds it is gone. White. Even our blacks go white. Stoking white coal, pouring white oil. . .

'My task?' asks Delia. 'I'm the creative type. In

science, nothing is made, you just discover. What a bore!'

'The ice cores,' says the captain. 'A sampler, tube, long a mile. . . We ream right down. And what you find is ashes. Ancient fires. Peach pits, and peacock crests. Brass door knobs, whisks of elephant hair; and kebab swords, birch-bark scrolls with villanelles. . . You log it in, you write it down, you warm them up, and lock them into drawers – and you keep schtum. Nothing must leak out of how this was the happy land, sun and equality, palaces of porphyry and malachite. Useless to tell the world how in a night – it all transformed. The ice queen, Bluebeard, vampires – all that crap – imprisonment, deep freezing, coldflying things – maybe doves flapped off with legends of the place . . . and then it stopped. Frosted for ever. A few tall tales of night and dark, and blizzards at the door, that's all. And sank. And crumbled into drifts – a massive heap of junk like Oxyrhinkus. Just left some walruses, sluglike and legless on the floes: some flightless birds who couldn't make it off. . .

'So, Delia,' the captain says, 'are you with us? Are you in the crew, and will you dance, and cheer along, and boost for German movies, and the golden age that gelid lies beneath our keel?'

'It's most attractive,' Delia says. 'I see how we must

hide the history of what there was, and all the good folk frozen in their beds, the silence and the fluting of the wind, the land that has no reeds, no nymphs, no gods, no piping at midday. . .'

'Oh, we could pipe,' the captain says, 'if that's what you'd most miss. The notes would freeze in cubes – we'd put them in your drink and as you sipped they'd thaw and disappear, "cube after cube" we'd call the piece . . . .'

*

'You've left your cloak,' Regina says. 'This new one – black and white – the arms are short. Those orange slippers . . . cute!'

'I'm sceptical about the science,' Delia says. 'I was shown deep down. And sworn to secrecy. I think we may all end bad.'

'You don't need to discover gravity to know that,' Regina says. 'You need protection, Delia, not the algebra.'

'Doctor Gritt,' says Delia, 'believed in slavery. Done right, of course – loyalty reciprocal, all that. My sister Masha should have stayed with him – it's drift, Regina, if there's no one to look out for you. There's ice all round, and depths you must keep quiet about.'

Regina doesn't understand all that: she says, 'We know the problems people here have said they face – the trees, and those poor papagayos. Doubtless other worries too. . . There's hundreds of those Doctor Gritts, will tell them how to solve the lot. But – we have problems too. Who will solve ours? The sisters from the settlements – they're angry, and they're armed. We'll have to parley, Delia. Semyon – will find some Russians, those are everywhere. I know them like I know my hand – a hand's a hand, not much to know. . . There'll be a church, a network – faith and fiddle, that's for sure. But you, dear Delia? Not more than my half-sister . . . too bad, this country isn't like your hope. . . The roads here seem to go for ever, then they disappear, without a destination, in a sandy pond. . .'

'Analyse, Regina!' Delia says. 'I can be Mélisande, but don't cast yourself as Pelléas.'

'Of course, Delia,' Regina says. 'No touching. That's the rule. We don't have many options, though: stealing perroquets and iguanas. Or – exotic dance.'

'I've a bad experience up the trees,' says Delia. 'And for exotic dance – we'd need a room.'

'Your Doctor Gritt would have got us funds,' Regina says.

'Don't get him wrong,' says Delia. 'He believed in

slavery, it's true. His team, the quest – seeking El Dorado . . . Behind slavery . . . in front, I mean, there was the ideal. Saving the world, or making it live longer. Like for the Greeks – it was democracy.'

'We could practise here,' Regina says. 'Titillation – a teasing dance, it's maybe alien to the culture. We can try it in the road.'

No one stops. Semyon applauds. There's no sex,' he says. 'At least – no promise, not of anything. Just the dance – like in the picture – red bodies, a green ground. It's perfect for this place – but you may not see it so. You'll need a niche, for your niche audience.'

'Oh no,' Regina says. 'We need thousands. Hideyholes. Cash: my ambition is scientific – I'll start up the experimental life again – disarmed this time.'

'Lots try dance,' says Semyon. 'Our bodies – we have freed them. It's our minds – still stuck on the old track – dissatisfaction. Imagination lasts a lifetime – the real thing is frittered in a night.'

'Bare feet, Delia,' Regina says, doing something complicated with a lilt and slide. 'Take off those flippers. There's a bit of monkey about you – that's good. Keep the Dominican robes – that's class. . .'

'No!' says Delia, weeping. 'It won't raise cash. How I miss Masha – she knew how to behave.'

'You lack gravitas,' Semyon says. 'Is this the best you can do? Having seen the abyss, all that?'

'I was scarcely nurtured,' Regina says. 'So I must rely on nature.'

'It's true for me too,' says Delia. 'Though it may seem casuistry.'

'You were more natural in feathers,' Semyon says. 'But people here have made a business out of dancing. Try something else – or emigrate.'

*

Ben. He held it all together. He made it fly apart. You can fawn on him, not talk to him. What do you want to say, anyway? It's all a crazy scheme, in a crazy place – people who object to being led, accept a leader. Throw him out. Don't know what to do – nothing to do with him. Or anyone similar to Ben, even if they're all like that – born, elected, riding in – they hold it all together and they make it fly apart.

'I photo well,' Regina says: 'I could do what Ben did. Get thrown out. Or do it better: get to build my mausoleum, and to lie in it.'

'Those vipers, scorpions?' Delia asks. 'Those sisters, brothers? Those we ran from? Though – it's true – I miss that stand of trees, the old, old man, his wisdom, the advice, the weedy garden he forgot to water. . .'

'No, Delia,' Regina says. 'We need some different people, maybe a far-off place. The dancing – gets us used to crowds. Your suit – gives a monastic tinge, the simian paws – a feel of frolicking beneath the covers. Mmmm – I love a guy in uniform, even if he's a fare collector on the trams. I'm sure it works the same for you. . . We'll find a way to silence Ben, make it easy for him, our bro, shake his tree, sail him off, find him a breeze! I'll be queen bee, and you're my chief inquisitor. "The Happy Land" – that's our device.'

The Gorgon – the gap-toothed mask, half smile, half retch . . . they both think 'That's what we'll put on coins.'

Regina's homely – full length, a little dumpy, and too short. Her smile – the Happy Land must not seem sugary. A profile? Or straight-faced? Too ordinary. . . 'You could be veiled,' says Delia. 'That would be a novelty on coins.'

'On notes, maybe,' Regina says. 'The coins – we'll throw them from our chariots. "Silver and steel", our cars, the poem says – that's taste, the Waldorf, Delia. That way, we'll bring happiness to us, to them. . .' They laugh, already whirling with the fantasy, they spin like gorgon coins flipped to the sky, before a match.

'Oh yes,' says Semyon. 'How I know that urge! '*Il*

faut tenter de vivre,' they say. You're wrong, Regina, you're misled, in the wrong game – they tell you it takes courage to persist in error. Courage? So what? See things clear, and true, that takes intelligence, the chances are you only see mistakes – and someone stupid but determined will come to do you down; refined doubters, they're pushed aside, or underground. . .'

'No, Semyon,' Regina says, 'I'm bright enough to use stupidity. Error doesn't enter this. I don't deal in belief or plausibility. We'll put the Gorgon's head on both sides of the coin. That way we'll always win a toss. . .'

She practises the grin: her oft-circulated face – is a gorgon worth more than Ben, a jeton – leaning on his oak stump, aloft his club, the lion's skin. . . ?

And Semyon – tall and pale, grey potin, a tallow candle. 'How often have we seen such guys, their fuses lit, smouldering on the ramp, ready to bring the fire and racket over us – and others,' Delia thinks.

Regina knows to rise up from their poverty: they must get power. Beauty comes in second place. It means replacing Ben. Allying. Making friends and enemies.

'Of course,' Regina says. 'When we have found our spot, we'll need Semyon's mates. They're disciplined. . .'

'What's behind it, Regina,' Delia asks. 'The power you seek? Understanding, or chrism? Seeing clear, or having the gift, the urge?'

'I don't know,' Regina says. 'And that's not cynical. I just don't know. I guess that means that revelation gives you understanding. No either-or. Ask Semyon – he and his friends – they're experts. That way, go with them, and philosophy's resolved.'

'This is all new to me,' says Delia. 'Science, what I did – is starts; there is no stop. Your Happy Land, though, Regina – navigates among the rocks, it's a hiatus, the cog's missed tooth, the wheel that turns and spins and does not catch. A fortune that you spend at once that leaves you no more wise. . .'

'Decide!' Regina says. 'Are you with me, or in the tree, dressed in the feathers. . . ?'

*

'Of course you're right,' says Delia to herself. 'Regina is no sister. Why should I play along, her plan – making the rich poor, the poor rich? You're a scientist, Delia, your material's as old as stones, but what you make of it – is new. That is the artistry. . . I'm a Phidias. Doctor Gritt says the cash you get is for the contribution you have made – unless the money's stolen. If it wasn't so, the poor would take their money from the rich, instead of struggling on – maybe there's always someone in between, that keeps them both apart. . . I've not contributed much here, not anything – I'm last in, first out. Furio the fixer says he'd fetch me, but can't find me on his map. Oh Masha, if I'd an address, you'd write to me. . . '

'There's not much here now,' Regina says. 'Except lots of people. Then there's the ladders – politics, Delia. We're the snakes – up we go!'

'It used to be a place of magic,' Delia says. 'Every tree, a soul – they'd come down and dance. . .'

'That happens still,' says Semyon. 'Concentrate on the ladders, Delia. They're slippery, not like trees.'

'Ben – I want to see him climb and fall,' says Delia. 'Then, I might be with you, Regina.'

'Oh, he doesn't climb, and so you won't see him fall,' Regina says. 'Vendetta doesn't suit you, Delia.'

'Suit or not,' says Delia. 'I'm off. He did me bad.'

'It's in the culture, dear,' Regina says, impatiently. 'There's no Happy Land without some tears.'

'Revenge? It isn't me,' says Delia. 'But I shall study it. And act.'

'It isn't possible,' Regina says, 'to settle all the scores. There's yours, and Masha's. Is that the secret of the world? It's eyes for eyes?'

'Maybe it's not everything,' says Delia. 'Change, stability – those are part of it. Vendetta. It petrifies, but also sweeps away. It's reason, not intelligence. It makes sense – but maybe you should ignore that. . . Of course, its aim is justice.'

Regina says. 'Why don't you stay, work for the proletariat. . . Your shamanism – that was just a cloak dropped on your nakedness.'

'I know,' says Delia. 'Shamanism needs your wits. I have no secrets. It's all bets. Pretending you know how things will turn out. The working class, Regina? Oh, that would be serious. I'm not serious, you know, Regina. I've my doubts about you too. I'll study the vendetta – its rules, its longevity, the satisfactions that it doesn't bring. Its rules, its canons and its codes – how it binds the centuries. . . Old time – gives blood to all that's new. . .'

*

'Ben,' Regina asks, 'What did you do to Delia?'

'No touching,' Ben says. 'The truth.'

'You shouldn't have done that, Ben,' Regina says, 'What made you?'

'The reed she can't play!' says Ben: 'My ears! I told her all her future – how she was second-rate, a mark. No qualities. How Masha's not a sister – not to her, and not to anyone.'

'You and I,' Regina says, 'We can do deals. Go easy on the truth. Delia's off, to prove you wrong. Why does she care? We'll find a ladder, you and I. . .' and off they go together. . .

*

'Regina was my sister, Masha,' Delia says. 'But I could say now – I hate her. Her aim. The power, the politics – first, it's done to live. Then, to appear. I've not come to the open, Masha. Ought I? Ben and Regina – theirs is a big continent – there are people angry everywhere, wanting to be led, and following after other things that's hard to find. . . Feuding societies – that's what I'm studying here. We'll do some science, Masha, you and I, meanwhile. I'll think how I can undo the hurt. . .'

'There's no trees here,' says Masha, looking round. 'Unless you count the stunted oaks, those cork trees up amongst those ancient stones. . . You might count the sheep – that's what they do, and sleep all day . . . and in the evening, drink. Remember. That's all there is, there is no present here. And they hate, Delia, just like you.'

'I see the sheep,' says Delia. 'I hear the shepherds

sleeping, chuckling in their dark. But there's bullet-holes in all the signs. They kidnap, Masha, they do drugs and sell them on, and they keep schtum, just like we'll have to do if we discover awkward science, wavering in the galaxy. . .'

The rule here in the village is – don't point. That's Masha's big advantage, as she can't.

'Everyone eats that flatbread with fried eggs,' says Delia. 'That must account for something. It sets inside you, like the Roman concrete – within, you are granitic . . . a dull quartz. . .'

The house they live in is built round a tree – every village has a house like that. You can carve a ghoulish mask from the wood, make it a drum, or stretch a string across. At night, that you can use the trunk to climb from floor to floor. The branches are stubby, but it's time, not life, that makes them grow, then become cumbersome.

'Do you hear people outside when I'm asleep?' Masha asks. 'Tapping on the door? Maybe I'm a scaredy type, but I'm afraid of kidnap. The shepherds don't sleep in the fields with their sheep, cuddled together in the dark, but they drink all night, go to their little huts and sleep all day. There, Delia! you'll have all the time you want to seek revenge, evaluate an insult, see an enemy from afar. . .'

'We could analyse things here,' Delia says, not much enthused. 'The granite. The cork. The cheese.'

'Don't be angry, Delia dear,' says Masha, hanging clothes to dry on a branch, picking some fruit, bitter persimmons, that grow there. 'I'm your only sister now. It's all small stuff here – just families. Where there's countries involved, there's much more noise and movement. You get parcels too, and tents.'

'Yes, Masha,' Delia says. 'Perhaps that's what I seek. It's more normal, with aeroplanes and spies. Here, you see too much. It's like the Ramayana.'

'You don't see anything at all, Delia,' Masha says.

'That's what I mean,' says Delia. 'You see the branches, and the sky where the tree grows out; all that you know, and it goes no further, doesn't enter you or turn against and fall on you. But you don't see the people that come for you, or hide behind the wall with shotguns. . .'

'We'll analyse materials,' Masha says. 'Maybe they'll sell them better. Not that I care. The people'll probably ignore us. Have you decided, Delia, if revenge is nature? Or is it nurture? I can't wait for you to tell . . . Just watch our tree, calm in the house, walled in, no breeze, no one can fall from here.'

'There's danger all around,' says Delia. 'That's what I

like, because it's me that's safe.'

'You're right,' says Masha. 'Remember – with this feuding – there's no anger. It's routine, and satisfaction. When you repay the insult – you'll see how it'll please your mother. Bread and eggs, make you hard inside – I'll make you some right now, dear Delia, my sister. . . Toughen you up. . .'

*

There's reprisals. A nephew and his girl – there at the bus stop – she's snatched off, he gets blasted in the face. It's sad, they say: with more pauses, more divinity – you could say it is a tragedy. Just – be very, very careful. If it's theatre – no one's paid their ticket.

If you climb the tree, up at the top, out of the house – it's metaphor . . . but you can see down everywhere, see everyone, look in their beds, their ovens and their jars, and count their sheep, until you sleep. The tree bears fruit, and every day, Delia is wiser, and her rancour grows.

'Oh what the fuck,' says Masha. 'Brazil's so far away. Do you want revenge, dear Delia – or to make your point? You could send them poisoned cheese, I guess. . .'

'I owe a something to Alina,' Delia says. 'I feel it's

sisterhood betrayed, Ben and Regina, picking a team, flattering the acolytes – forgetting me . . . Making amends, Masha – is that the best? Each bears all human history within, no one's without the everything. Free will, destiny – they're in the pack that every infantryman and woman bears. We invented writing and it's spawn, eggs inside everyone, like on a keyboard, every word and every deed, everything is there, just waiting to be joined up and punctuated.'

'Furio,' says Masha. 'That's what you need. Have him climb up the tree, salute you, pretend to fecundate, and leave you satisfied. We know that he won't hang around. It must be someone from outside, or you'd fall in the net, they'll gift you sheep and lend you cash. . . You would be trapped, poor Delia . . . in for centuries, your name your misfortune. . . Your kids – janissaries. Even me, I'd be drawn in. . . !'

'My sister, Regina, and my brother, Ben, both taking it too easy,' Delia says. 'Getting thrown out. They'll run to here. Everybody knows, this is a hidden secret place. All the fugitives come here. We'll lie in wait. They'll never get away.'

'Well, Delia,' Masha says. 'They're harnessed to your cart, for sure. Now what? You cut a four-by-four, have it in readiness if they stumble on the track?'

*

'You've brought the garden inside the house,' says Ben: 'It's sterile, though . . . '

'Oh we can't have birds in here,' says Delia. 'This is where we do the science. There aren't so many substances around. There's no philosophy. For observation – we must be the birds, and climb up on the roof, peer down. We do the scientific work here where it's intimate – bedroom and kitchen, there's no window and we lock the door. . .'

'It's mostly bread and eggs,' says Masha, irritated. 'It's nurture, Ben. We see what there is in them, and then we have them for our meals. That's the best way.'

'Oh, we have news of Semyon,' says Regina, putting on her domesticity. 'He's into currency. The church was keen on substance, but he preferred a life more fluid, even abstract. . . '

'You're lucky that the people here are feuding types,' says Ben. 'In Brazil, we got thrown out because we loved the people, and we served them. In this village, they avoid us. Every shutter closed as we came up the strip. . .'

'Our project was to anticipate,' Regina says. 'You remember – accelerate! Do the history before it does for you. We had a group, a party, we were centuries ahead. . .'

'They said we were not worthy, lazy, drunk. . .' says Ben.

'Oh Ben,' Regina says, voice in a break, 'don't mention the humiliation! Semyon will send us cash. . .'

'Seeing you so pitiful,' says Masha, 'makes me think – I shan't harm you, shan't pursue the feud – no whip, no anger . . . after all, Delia's the one who suffered. . . '

'Suffered?' shouts Regina. 'You sisters ought to do philosophy. Speculate, investigate the order of the universe. That's what sisters should be for – not poking at your food, sitting atop the trees, your heads off in the swim.'

'It's so,' says Delia. 'I lost my sister. Alina fell. I got fed up with Doctor Gritt, his dream of immortality. Is he immortal? It's too soon to tell. The same goes for the sun. It is unlikely it can last beyond my death, but the laboratory – it makes you think it all is possible – draining the world to make it habitable, and grow our food all over. . . There's no end in sight. . . And Semyon's cash can buy us all a pause in blood feuds. We could live here in peace, and barricade the place – the villagers give up so easily. We aren't their kind.'

'The happy land?' asks Masha.

'That's still there,' says Ben. 'Now, where'll we all sleep tonight?'

'Three sisters in a bed,' says Delia. 'If Furio comes he can sleep with Ben.'

'It's not like families I have known,' says Masha. 'Remember that play about the bird? That's where I belong: I say, "I'm in mourning for my life. I'm unhappy. It isn't a question of money. Even a poor man can be happy."'

'Furio?' asks Regina. 'Never heard of him. Is he the poor man? What's he to do with Ben?'

'We'll hear him banging on the door,' says Delia. 'He came to pleasure us, but we can wait.'

'Our research,' says Masha, 'should be towards a cure – for unhappiness. Like in the theatre. . .'

'You cretin,' Regina shouts. 'That was our scheme. You can't patent it.'

'It means you have to choose the people,' Masha says, 'The ones you're easy with. Cut out the rest. Like – your sister, Delia – Alina was the intrusive kind.'

'Let's all drink this Canonau,' says Delia. 'In the name, you have a cannon and a canon – that's a start.. Offence, defence. . .'

'A start for nothing, Delia,' Ben shouts at her. 'We made the trek to get here, liven you both up, and find a refuge. . . But here you are, both miserable, confined. You missed your chance, Delia – you should have taken ship, followed the albatross, shot it down, resolved unhappiness – all that. Remember, Masha, "all lives, all lives, having accomplished the sad cycle, have been extinguished". That goes for Delia's horse as well. Let it fall. Hold your four-by-four: if it dies, it'll do so without your help. "This poor moon lights its lantern in vain" – we tramped towards extinction, along with all the pretty beasts. Then – that was the mission, Masha, Delia – a philosophy that will go beyond, that leaves the world on – as they say – the cusp of immortality, so, at our death – it's there! It lives! It buries us! It says good things about us, and our work, elides our personalities, our mistakes. Makes us – almost all – the good guys of the epic! Well, if Furio comes – I'll not have him in my bed. Some things, some people – they are out! Forget the guys that prowl outside – if this guy Furio shows up – I'll not have him in my house!'

'Our house!' says Delia.

'Exactly, Delia,' Regina says. 'Our house.'

'Our eggs, our bread, our sun,' says Delia. 'Our life.'

'Stuck here,' says Ben, 'you don't remember what countries your lot's at war with!'

'We all have different countries, or have none,' says Masha. 'Mine has all different kinds within – some fight each other now, and others maybe will.'

'This Canonau is good and strong,' says Ben.

'The thing is,' Masha says, ignoring him and drinking up, 'is being with people who are good. Good to you. If there are such, and if you find a team of them, and – there you are. You can't go on with people who can't stand you.'

'All that,' Regina says, 'we've been through. This is the second time we didn't suit. Maybe there's a problem with the chief. With Ben.'

'It's not being chief,' says Ben, quite irritated. 'You're brothers all your life, and sisters. Brothers, sisters, as it falls. Then there are strangers, that you love. Now, your average cat or dog – they'll love you all their lives, and when the euthanasia moment comes – they trust you. You've the key – you've always had it. Even if there's sheep or cows, and in the end you eat them – the feeling is the same, at least, it is for them. Your lovers end up indifferent, or hating you. But sisters – they go on and on. That's curious.'

'This Furio,' Regina says, 'I don't see him fitting in. We could do something with the beds, and have me, Regina, in with Ben, the sisters in the other. This knocking on the door – we know it's Furio. He'll go away, in time. No one will stop him. There's no danger for him, unless he's snatched. And we're at peace now, we four, no rancour, and no conflicts.'

'How goes Brazil?' asks Delia, trying to lighten up.

'It goes up and down for sure,' says Ben. 'But it was marked out by the pope. That's a great start.'

'Show us the mask they wear here,' Regina says. 'My! It's so smooth it could be plastic.'

'We only wear it so's they don't spy on us,' says Masha. 'Shopping. If you put horns on top, the meaning's clear. Otherwise – it's the holy spirit – or it could be a woman's face, that's how they see things here. The women don't sing along. . . The boys have choirs. . .'

There's no comment. The tree rubs against the floorboards – they may be sisters too.

'I don't hate you, Ben,' says Delia, otherwise at a loss. He grunts.

'This Furio – if it's for sex he comes, he sounds degenerate,' Regina says.

'He spreads tales of Doctor Gritt, his systems, and his wins. And he brings our cash,' says Masha. 'Often he doesn't come, sometimes he stays.'

They sleep. The moon sleeps with Endymion, Ben sleeps with Masha. It's not a great idea.

'There's riches here,' says Ben. 'I smell them.'

'I'll shake the tree,' says Delia. 'I heard them in the night – the birds: the weakest ones get pushed out the nest. The others lay their eggs. . . Best be rid of those on land, not drop them in the sea, or on the ice. . .'

'That's all mixed up,' says Masha. 'These birds are going to Brazil. This is a stop-off. Eggs is a bother. A pregnant bird's a bigger shape, you might get shot.'

'I'll make eggs for you all the same,' says Delia. 'Ben's right. They bring it in, the dope, at night, in dinghies from the yachts. Doctor Gritt gets funds from that, and sends his Furio. . .'

'Don't drop all your eggs at once, dear Delia,' Masha says, angry.

'Your Doctor Gritt's a libertarian,' says Ben. 'Although he makes his profits from the law.'

'Oh no,' says Delia. 'He's a Nobel. It's how they get their funds – the pills. He's great, whichever ways it drops. It's just the work with him is dull.'

Everybody nods – they've all known boring work.

It's hard to hate Ben, hungover, in his underwear.

'You could make the dope here,' Ben says.

There's a pile of dirty alembics, for testing cheese.

'The guys here . . . well,' says Masha, pretending to cut her throat with a long knife. 'They can get you sent to jail – it's by the shore. You see the dinghies coming in – a spectacle, but I'm too short to reach the view.'

'That way,' Regina says, 'we'd never need to leave. In

jail or in the lab – we'd be a family.'

'I could buy a gold ring,' Masha says, 'with a tree of life. The Seljuks used it – maybe they were Jewish, some of them. It symbolises love. The Seljuks believed in take it easy, Brother Charlie – but in love as well. Yes, Ben, love, courting: not a jostle in the dark.'

'We could all buy gold rings,' Ben says. 'And fall in love with whom we please. It won't last, though. Doctor Gritt should open up some skulls and find out why.'

'That's all been lost,' says Masha. 'No passion. Just guns and running.'

'Oh Masha, what a hoot!' says Delia, distressed, trying to laugh it off. 'Gun-running! What a thought!'

'I'm all for dope,' says Ben. 'If it makes you spin. But guns is far more serious. If oil is politics, guns is – religion. Not in our settlements, please!'

'We could take on Semyon,' Regina says. 'He'd launder all our wealth – no need to hang it on the branches here, to dry.'

'How droll you are, Regina,' Delia says. 'I can't think now why I hated you – it must be Ben, the pacifier. . . Nothing annoys like being told a truth, when you have a seething fit. War, peace – pardon, reconciling. . . Forgetting, starting over: shaking hands and digging graves. . . Brass bands! We could have a state here, with a flag, a bank. The hayseeds here – how they would gape! We'd be class, Masha, have a zoo, gold rings on our hands and feet. Glass cladding round the tree . . . a feature in a mag. . .'

'You'd need the recipe from Doctor Gritt,' Regina says. 'You could make pills from chalk but . . . no! Best offer a hideyhole for him and Furio. . . They could live here. . .'

'Oh absolutely not,' says Masha. 'We're a family. And they'd cheat us. There would be sex, and empty bottles dropped in the street. . .'

'Doctor Gritt,' says Delia, 'gave us energy abundant, inexhaustible. And so – it ruined all the former places of supply . . . the oil, the rivers – useless. . .'

'Of course,' Regina says. She stands, cock of the forest. 'That's where we slipped. We took it easy – but the followers . . . they had free energy, and abundance of all its use. . . They wanted new cities, cosmology, new scripts. It all began to change. We – we were still infected by the old disease: happiness. We wanted an experiment. We thought it would turn out well – for us. It was like the Maya had returned – no happy land, rather, a golden age. A succession of new ideal forms – kings and nobles, human sacrifices – our pets paraded, some to the butchers, others worshipped, mostly both. . . Divinities were imminent, we all had doubles – animals and lesser gods. Everything was sorted into hierarchies . . . even the branches and the grass, the serpents . . . trees that reached to heaven. . . Inventions without end. We hadn't thought.. One day it was formalism, next – romantics blowing conches. We didn't modernise, couldn't accommodate to all the change. They left us far behind. Moral police, the puritanism, you could only use five words for everything, desire and abnegation arm in arm. . . The bombing planes they wanted, then the shelters – did you hear the bangs? The forest Indians – the worst. Militias, my dears . . . the bodies left unburied . . . chewed by jaguars. . .

'Then – the crises that they couldn't handle. The despots and the anarchists – the diets and the wildfires. . . Poor useless Ben, poor Brother Charlie . . . chased out, expelled, not for wisdom this time, but for ignorance.'

'It all began with Doctor Gritt,' says Ben. 'He ruined us. Now he must build us up again. . .'

'Take it easy,' Masha says. 'It hasn't happened, Ben.'

'Of course, I've speeded it all up,' says Ben. 'Our settlement was just a taste. The guys we had recruited – they lived it all in quick, quick time. What can we do? I thought of sacrifice. The sacrifice of Doctor Gritt – but it's too late.'

'Dope,' Marsha says, 'that slows it down, slows

everything. Guys want their good time, but – no happyland, no golden age. Forgetfulness. . . That gives us pause. No tree that reaches to the sky, no hierarchy, no other side, no heaven with your enemies poised and waiting for you – no spirit guides . . . no cops.'

'It's our buried future. An archaeology to come. No place for us. And do we want it – the land where we don't belong?' Regina asks. No one responds. Ben – he seems to cry.

*

'Don't be distressed, Masha,' Delia says, when they're alone. 'That future – if it comes, we'll never know. The people – they're not happy, but they're satisfied. They're doing right – the trouble is, dear Masha, you've been persecuted, so you've become a hedonist. Did you want me all, all for yourself? And are you happy now?'

'Come, Delia,' Masha says. 'We've analyses to do. That cheese – can cure a broken leg. . .'

Delia climbs the tree – it's thrown a spike of blooms, white, a sugary drip. There's the stones the primitives had stood on end, over beyond the little oaks. 'It just grows,' thinks Delia. 'Sometimes it dies. It's us, staring in the mirror – we think it's beautiful, nature – we don't think we are, until we're chiselled in white stone, maybe lose a nose, a penis, arms and breasts. That's lovely, we are not. I'm covered in a rash, like cherry pits. Maybe it's the drink. I need to shear my nose-hair. . .'

'Stop looking at yourself, Delia,' Masha shouts up. 'Come down and help.'

'We all miss our sisters,' Regina says. 'Even when they're close at hand. Nature's no substitute, however hard we look. . .'

'Don't confuse her, Regina,' Masha says. 'Nature is better than a pill. It doesn't work as well, but does less harm.'

'I'll stay up here,' Delia shouts down. 'It's mine, my territory,' and she squawks.

'It's too dangerous,' Masha says. 'I don't want to run some more – not with the trafficking I've had – how many more times. . . ?'

'We're running now,' shouts Delia. 'We always will.'

Masha throws out all the glass – it makes a shriller sound than bottles breaking in the street. 'There!' shouts Masha. 'It's resolved. Oh Delia – I'm a spy. That's why I always get what I desire. Now, I have you, Delia – I want nothing more.'

'That's over, Masha,' says Regina. 'There's no need now to be ashamed. . . '

'I'm not,' says Masha. 'I've always been a spy most excellent. You need them, spies and traitors – otherwise everything would always last for ever.'

'I studied vengeance, Masha,' Delia shouts. 'Maybe I should study you. What might occur. . .'

'That's rhetoric,' says Masha. 'Shows you haven't understood. I have no rest, that's all. No one pursues me, that I know. I drew you in . . . being unique, Delia. . .'

'I love hearing how you sisters meet,' Regina says, not knowing where she's at.

'Come down, Delia, or I'll shake the tree,' shouts Masha. 'You'll end up on the retorts out in the street.'

'You're a betrayer, Masha,' Delia says, and weeps.

'I spied, that's all,' says Masha. 'I do it now, like everyone. Delia – I put you in my cage, you're safe. The animals – they accept a loss. They lose their siblings – no vengeance, and no tears. Humans – they too must accept the loss. There's nothing else. I'll protect you, Delia, if I can. If you don't like it, break the bars. Fuck off.'

*

'That glass!' says Ben. 'It tells all. More than all! You think you broke it – but in that instant – you're revealed! You're in my frame, Delia and Masha, like it or not!

Suspicion is enough – the guys here will believe we're all complicit. To them, it's clear what you do – clearer than what you really do. Everyone knows what you're compounding. Even if you aren't.'

'It's true,' Regina says. 'They spy on you: the glass – that's a giveaway, they'll soon see through you both. . . It turns the vision, picture, that they have of you, your image, innocence – turns it around. Throwing the glass – it shows you up. You're hide and seekers now!'

'Look,' says Ben. 'We're in an awkward scene. I'll cook some dope, and then we'll run. We've the universe, all space, to hide us in.'

'I didn't realise you knew the trade,' Regina says.

'Oh, I picked it off TV,' says Ben. 'I'll need these scientists to fill the details, and the glass.'

*

Golden Age
Is what they call the pills.

'You'll kill our tree,' says Masha, 'pouring the waste around the roots. Heaven – it's going up, up to heaven! See how it lifts the birds – the leaves, burnished splendid, brassy, the sun hits, makes them a mat of golden stars, and in the night. . .'

'Yes,' Delia says. 'At night they glow – acetylene, the waves respond – night into day . . . with our electrum shine, they'll see us from the moon. . .'

'Delia,' says Masha, quite alarmed. 'Your head's gone lumpy. . .'

'Oh,' says Delia, 'I don't think they're horns – just my little Pan bumps. . .'

'The moon has horns,' says Ben. 'Maybe you're into that. . . I've often seen them in Brazil. . .'

'We're not going there again,' says Masha. 'It's not a happy land. But – my Golden Age is so far back – you've never seen things taken easier since. . . Who was I then, I ask? Brother? Sister? Amir, shepherd. . . Did I believe something of me would always live? Did I sit upon the ground and weep or on a golden chair and drink my wine and stroke my kestrel's head? Now – there's hypocrisy. And worse.'

*

You put the Golden Age gel on your lips – and when you're kissed, your partner spins off to their Age. If you're not kissed – that's just too bad. If you don't have a Golden Age – that's too bad too: you stay right where you are. Kissing the mirror – doesn't activate the molecules, it just leaves a smudge.

'It's a miraculous pharmakon,' says Ben, 'but lacks a universal coverage. I won't consult with Doctor Gritt until we've sorted out our paradise. Meanwhile – the guys here have to be cut in. That's difficult – they've always kept their sheep – millennia! There is no Golden Age for them – not one to come, nor in the past. . . They think we're charlatans. . .'

'My tree!' says Delia. 'The tree-house with Alina – that was the best of all my possible worlds.'

'I was in a bar just now,' Regina says, 'and was lifted off my feet – laughing, they said I should prepare for kidnap. . .'

'That's fantasy,' says Ben. 'It's for the tourists. We don't do this for the cash – it's for building other settlements, for living right. And paying everybody off – and there'll be Gritt, his royalties. . .'

'You don't listen,' Delia shouts. 'What if the tree dies?'

'Nature-nurture? Is the brain hard-wired?' Regina shouts back – 'Are those your problems? I tell you, I'm terrified. . .'

'If we were mad,' says Delia, 'those problems would be a solution. Something to work from. . .'

'You *are* mad. And they aren't,' Regina says. 'It's your characters that's wrong.'

'It's fear,' says Masha. 'We'd be more interesting if there wasn't. . .'

'It's never the person, it's what they make happen to them,' says Ben. 'If you don't wish it all, you can't wish for anything better.'

*

The tree shivers, twists, its bark makes faces, its arms writhe. It happens slowly, so you don't see, until it's finished. 'Wonderful,' says Delia. 'It's what we made. We'll leave now.'

'It's true,' says Masha. 'The tree's organic, just like us. But there it stands . . . useless, it seems, now dead. . . It's me you see there, Delia, up through the middle of our house.'

'I think,' says Ben, 'I'll make the settlers ingest the balm, instead of smearing it. That way – who knows? – they'll maybe always live the Golden Age. . .'

'That's not the point,' says Masha. 'Dope is made so there is an after and before. That's why you take it. Otherwise – you'd always be spaced out, like being super-drunk for ever. It would be our normality. Maybe it's what we always are already: without a glass, a power that watches and reflects – we're fixed without a fix . . . The Golden Age, if it were lived forever in your gut, makes you an idiot. Perhaps it confirms that you are always so.'

'Then let it be,' says Ben. 'Mine's an experiment.'

'It's the kissing,' Regina says. 'Too glycerine.'

'It's too ephemeral,' says Ben. 'Settlers. They must have the feeling all the time, the exaltation, or they're not living in a settlement, with walls, and people in and others you are bound to keep outside.'

'We'll give it to the shepherds here,' Regina says. 'They'll swallow, be in the paradise they never had and never lost. You two, Masha, Delia – you'd better leave. We'll take the cash, the tree is dead – there's nothing left.'

'I'll expel myself,' says Delia, 'not wait for anyone. I don't think this will ever be a paradise. My tree. . .'

'Forget the tree,' shouts Masha: 'I've been expelled from hell already! You don't go from there to paradise, I promise you. We're wanderers. That is the best. . .'

'My tree . . . my sister,' Delia sobs. 'Gone. There's no "best".'

'Experience, my dear – that's all that we can trust, and even then, not much. Some of us – we're not suited to a sister role,' says Masha. 'Not having parents is a help. I try. I'm the willing cuckoo, Delia.'

'Vengeance?' Delia says. 'We'll seek it, and be made to run. Feuds? – the divinities instructed us. It all comes down, down from the skies. We are not trustworthy, it's right we hate each other. From our warring come the metamorphoses – from humans into bamboo, laurel, reeds. We're in the trap, under the scythe; they cut us down, we're mulch. We're bogmen, fertilising swamp. Ben's settlements – they're camps, like when we started out in Africa – but with boutiques, and speeded up. Who'll breach the walls, Masha? Where would all the people go then, without a home, without a cent?'

'Heavy questions, Delia,' Masha says. 'We'll take the ferry, get out quick. Find us another tree, we'll sit and ponder, maybe train some hawks, a raven, to do the foraging for us in the woods.'

*

'This time,' says Ben. 'They'll listen, take me as a model for the whole. Too many people on a tortured land. My settlers will sort it out – the best, the most aggressive type. . . '

'So long as they don't fight, like the last times,'

Regina says: 'We'll need some powerful friends – then we're beholden to them. . .'

'If it's logically possible,' says Ben, irritated, 'then it can be done. Two scattery types, Delia and Masha here – they do the procedures automatically, and it turns out well. You don't need flakey Doctor Gritt to read the manual and make a righteous scene.'

He and Regina take what's valuable: 'When I've saved the world,' says Ben, in good spirits, 'I'll make it beautiful.'

'No,' says Regina, 'Back to front again.'

*

Masha and Delia – smear what's left of Golden Age all over: 'Ready for love,' says Delia, 'But not in the mood,' says Masha.

The Swabian emperor covered a man with honey – had a bear to lick him clean. It was an experiment. Some honey's an halucigen, they say. The Golden Age drips through your skin. You have a movie going on inside – quick, crowded, wheels and nakedness . . .

There's no Swabians where they land, Masha and Delia. Hard to find a house, a tree that holds it up, a central pillar, like the machinery in a mill for making flour or pressing iron. ‘Remember, Masha,’ Delia says. ‘The ode to joy, the poet and those two – *geliebten Schwestern*, a fun ménage à trois! . . . Is that what awaits us, Masha dear?’

‘Oh no!’ says Masha. ‘Women didn’t have their bodies then, and they were awfully bored. . . And Schiller – what embarrassment! High mind and shorts to wash. The spitting blood and rant of revolution. . . ! Besides, my dear – that was all invented. And the sex – short and brutish: then, there’s a slummock left snoring in your cot.’

‘You be the bear, Masha,’ Delia says. ‘I’ll be the emperor. We agree – there’s no man. You lick me off, and I’ll do for you. . .’

Almost at once, they find the house, in an abandoned village, supported by fig trees – bearing the big green kind, the yellowish, the purplish dark. Put a fence round the undergrowth – and you’ve a garden.

‘Mmmm,’ says Masha. ‘How we love figs, dear Delia.’

*

Ben’s not so fortunate. The settlers get religion. They don’t do drugs, and put him in a cage. ‘Cleanliness,’ they say. It’s better for him than the cops.

'Beauty,' says Regina. 'That will come – but you need be very careful, with those experiments. The settlers' camps – mean trouble for the parrots. And those tall, tall trees.'

'If they chase me out,' says Ben, 'I hope they do. I'll start again, somewhere else. It's true, science isn't going anywhere, but it does have wheels. Where's these guys' religion going?'

*

'We have everything,' Masha says. 'Let's deal with those weeds. Off with their heads! There's even a song about them.'

'We can't be pregnant,' Delia says. 'There's nothing more powerful than chemistry, we know, but even so. . .'

They sing the song, and weed. This could be their Golden Age, the squat. . . The power is free, thanks to Doctor Gritt. But there are many neighbours.

Masha and Delia – outside their garden, there is evil. Can they avoid it? Does Masha worry about Delia's well-being? Delia doesn't consider Masha's, and Masha – she can't point. Not to anything. They're paper boats.

Ben's quest – he's a complex person. In history already. He doesn't want to do good, he wants to see how, when it ends, it begins again.

Regina doesn't worry about complexity – getting to her end is what concerns her. But no one knows how they'll all work out – they're so impulsive, and they've many resources – forests, gardens, science. . .

Masha hasn't thought how people will come into their house to harvest the different kinds of fig.

Mmmm, everybody likes figs. . .

*

'These guys – they don't seem good or evil,' Delia says. 'It's just they occupy the house. They're bunked in every space.'

'They'll leave when the figs have gone,' says Masha, 'and the fields are stripped – that's where they work. We could live up on the roof till then – but the guys who speak my language – they're not the docile kind.'

'They must be good or evil,' Delia says. 'It's no good being bits of both, not if it's trust you want.'

'We could traffic them,' says Masha. 'I'd get my own back. That's what people do. But – there is danger: them – and who's already trafficking. The cops, maybe . . . productive forces. . .'

'Knowledge,' says Delia. 'That's our trump, the last

one. We could invent another kind of fig. A red one. Everyone talks up the apple – those are bland. A peppery fig. Cut it in half – there's a vagina! Your book, Masha, I bet it puts the blame on women and the pomegranate. We'll do something new. . .'

'My book?' says Masha, vaguely. 'I think it says we came by boat. . .'

'That's crap!' shouts Delia. 'Seas were invented at the last, to stop us making friends all over. Salt water! what idiocy – no fucking use at all. . .'

'A fig!' says Masha. 'It seems modest. We could do better, better than Doctor Gritt.'

'You mean – a movie?' Delia says. 'That would be fun! Birth of a Nation update? Doktor Mabuse – my favourite one. . . ?'

'The guys here, on our floor,' says Masha. 'They're all Africans. Indians – maybe they came by boat. Many Babylonians. Think, Delia! It all starts here. This is our chance to lay out rules. We need a founding text. It's not like Ben, the settlers all contaminated – racists and urbanists, doctors and witches. . . No, these guys here, scum of the fields they're called. . . We'll tell a tale that they can cling to. The history of the world before it has begun! We'll make our document, without divinities and prophecies. Let them eat figs, free, without recriminations.'

'I had my thing for Pan,' says Delia, uncertain.

'I'll show you what a pipe can do,' says Masha. 'Pan didn't study. A mimsy fluting . . . I'd instal those grand old cinema organs, as backing for our flick. Pan's sado-eroticism – hmmm. I don't hold with it – no revenger tragedies, thunder and doom. . . A drag. No, Doctor Gritt has shown the way. Sun and wind, and bio-foods. That way, we'll. . .' She pauses.

'You see!' says Delia. 'We'll end up as gods! Our movie everywhere, compulsory. The species – will go on and on, cheating, as it does . . . imagine, ignoring the good life – tequila worms, the porno robots. . .'

'You're so cheap!' says Masha. 'Banalities! We can make a different end. A euthanasia, perhaps. Asceticism. Nomads fed by ravens. . .'

'It's sterile,' Delia says. 'The only good thing is the stars. That's us.'

'The problem is,' says Masha, 'it takes scores to make a movie. Menus. There's the catering. The tunes. Keeping them all on our track. . .'

'"Take It Easy. . ."' Delia says. 'We must have that. That's my favourite too.'

'The thing is, Delia,' Masha says, 'we must agree, we two. . . Me – I find you all too chic. A little

“Bedonebyasyoudo”. A paddler. In socks, and beaming.’

‘Oh Masha,’ Delia says, hugging her, ‘I know you had hard times. But – don’t be a cynic. Don’t make stern rules – those are the first they break.’

‘Listen, Delia,’ Masha says, ‘you can’t have a first movie, a first book, where the two founders don’t agree.’

‘Oh yes,’ says Delia. ‘There’s Mani. The good, the evil – fighting it out – bounded by the cage, where we all live. . .’

‘It’s implicit in them all,’ says Masha. ‘It’s their drama. You want operetta.’

‘If a movie’s too onerous,’ says Delia, ‘what then? An equation? A rocket, space explorers – how many should we send?’

‘A capsule’s rather naff,’ says Masha. ‘Think instead – Schiller and the Universal History. . . ’

‘Oh,’ says Delia, ‘even for me, that’s too marshmallow. The universe – it hadn’t even been discovered then.’

‘Well,’ says Masha, ‘our inspiration’s lying sleeping on our floor. They’ll be gathering *zucchine* by the dawn.’

Hotter and hotter grows the house. Miasma. ‘We could recruit some guys. . .’ says Delia.

‘No,’ Masha says. ‘Those all have doctorates. They’re good at maths. They’ll push us out.’

'People,' says Delia, 'they are everywhere. Too many – here, there's women too. Maybe we could put a stop to some of it? Think "mosquitoes". They've all gone, though. It's torrid here. . . Doctor Gritt's invention – conditioned air: it doesn't work so well, or else it works far better than we thought.'

'We need these guys to grow the food we eat. It must be cheap, because we have no cash, and they must eat as well,' says Masha.

'You're lecturing!' shouts Delia. 'That leads to cutting up those animals, pinned on the bench – you should know, you lost your index so!'

'It all connects,' says Masha, 'although you mustn't think of that. If we're all one, we're all complicit. . .'

'You spied!' shouts Delia. 'Probably did worse.'

*

On the roof, on different trees, the sisters sit.

'Who wants to rule the world,' says Delia, hoping Masha hears, 'when it's so easy to control?'

The guys beneath, the gatherers, stir. There's squads of them, unarmed, courageous, swirling together, ready for the vegetables, like starlings: those skyparades, plumping and withering – motoring veils or strawberry nets – up they go! ‘Oh, don’t ask why!’ says the song, an auspice.

‘Enough with those five-colour maps,’ says a guy below the sisters, pausing on the stoup: ‘Each bird, they tell us, keeps its post referring to just seven others, who it doesn’t need to know. In the speed, it couldn’t recognise them anyway – they could be brothers, uncles – it doesn’t matter which they are, or strangers. Like they say – perfect strangers. How do you know that it’s perfection? You suppose it is, and so must we. . .’

‘Go away,’ shouts Delia. ‘Leave our house!’

‘The birds have eaten everything,’ the guy, the mathematician, says. ‘We’ll follow them, on our one-colour map . . . over the sea, the useless sea. . .’

‘You’re wrong,’ says Masha. ‘The sea is useful. Doctor Gritt – put a bridle on it. A white horse.’

The guys – no one answers, they run from the fields, dumping their flipflops in the dust, kicking over the boxes of red pepperoni curled like boxing gloves – run to the sea, jump in the dinghies. Oh no! The sea! Again! No discount for the first time. . . We’re so low down, we can see its eyes, up and down they go. Make the journey back to Africa, where they say everyone began. ‘An empire,’ they shout, ‘An empire of Kobes, hard men. So! Pick your own fucking vegetables. . .’

'They're right,' says Masha to Delia. 'But down there, it's the women who do everything – the men'll lounge around like you, Delia. You're soft. Nothing has ever happened to you. You're fixated on your Doctor – Gritt, Mabuse. . . those deal from the bottom of the pack . . . ruling the world, as if. . .'

'Oh no, Masha,' Delia says. 'We all got a fritware plaque, the whole team. That's what happened. It was a challenge for us engineers. It doesn't conduct. It showed us. We can't go anywhere, you realise – the earth, the stone, everything we stand on – it's all inert. It's dead. Worms, Masha, that's all that comes out of it. They say Doctor Gritt – cheated at cards. Maybe you're right, Masha: when he'd invented everything – that is the end. Nothing's left. All that current released – burning us up. Like poor Ben – they covered him in jelly, in the cage: they burned him up.'

'That's terrible, Delia, if it's true,' says Masha, disbelieving her.

*

Regina arrives, juiced up with the news. 'Ben,' she says, 'He crackled, at the end. Drugs, politics – where could it go? Politics, drugs, I guess. The settlers covered him with gel – no golden age: – petroleum. 'You can't just sleep around,' they said: 'A polished bone – that is your inspiration. And your destiny.' And then,' she says, wept out, 'The fire. The wind. For what was left – the earth. So. . . What have you done, Delia, Masha, my lovely sisters. . .'

'Nothing,' says Masha. 'We thought. And so we quarrelled.'

'Nothing,' says Delia: 'We planned. More food, or more knowledge? Either way, we thought we'd be speeding up the end.'

'This house is beautiful,' Regina says: 'So empty. And so bare. The trees – why, it's not a house at all, it's trees. . .'

'The Africans ran off,' says Delia. 'They saw it was as bad here as where they'd left. And here, they had a boss to spur them. . . So – nothing. That was their choice. Empire, or shipwreck. They are in the waves.'

'Is life better if it's difficult?' Regina asks. 'It's hard to tell. It isn't written down. We're lucky, having one life to get on with. Imagine if you had to think of thousands. Poor Ben – he knew how it should be . . . the everything. . .'

'We had an honour,' Delia says, trying to lift the mood: 'Poor Doctor Gritt, the card-sharp – is disgraced, but all the team got this. . .' And she brings out the plaque, the frit, glazed, impervious to all electric things – except for time, that makes a *craquelure*. . .

‘That’s lovely,’ Regina says: ‘And Masha didn’t get a recognition, nothing – she can’t even point accusingly. . .’

‘We’re here, three sisters,’ Masha says. ‘Full of potential – wasted here.’

*

‘A memorial?’ Delia suggests.

‘For Doctor Gritt, we thought The Gamblers. But it didn’t fit,’ says Masha. ‘I only know the chorus, but we’ll do that for Ben – ‘Take It Easy’. That’s a sure bet.’

There’s a reading too. ‘“I remember the laughter, noise, shooting, and love-making” – Yes,’ Regina says. ‘That’s Ben, that’s how it was. “You should not sit in the country, it’s a sin” – that’s us three . . . There’s hope! Masha, with your talent, Delia – your sensibility – we’ve dodged the obstacles, no one has been hurt, no skeletons in closets. Ashes. . .’

‘Ben was a good man, Regina,’ Delia says. ‘Does anybody doubt it? Is that enough? Masha was so good to me when my other sister died – I wasn’t close at all, not to Alina.’

‘It isn’t easy to be good here, where we are,’ Masha

tells Regina. 'Not that anyone cares. You don't pick countries, or your sisters, after all. We've been part of great things, Regina. Helping the species, saving it to have another try. It's like driving a Ferrari made of jello. . .'

'We could open a boutique,' Regina says: 'We have the culture. Mirror the world in clothes – then break the glass, step from behind the curtain: real, ourselves, without adornment. Naked. Be respected, honoured.'

'Of course,' says Delia, 'That's all topside. Ben, us – saving the world, or cutting it a crutch – it's the imperial dream, without the flashy flags and topees.'

'"Serve the people" Delia, surely you've heard of that,' says Regina, angry. 'Don't start that settler talk with me – humility got no one nowhere.'

'Opening a boutique,' Masha says. 'Where does that fit with the cosmology? Those Africans – indifferent to our frocks. They wanted colour, the only thing we lacked.'

'It's your past, Masha,' Delia says. 'Stops your frolic. Your sect. . . A thundercloud. We'll buy stuff in. . .'

'Delia, you're spoilt,' shouts Masha: 'We're all in sects. To save myself, I died. Is there more to say? My finger went so there'd be no need to point – just make a fist. . . '

'Oh Masha,' Delia says. 'Poor dear. . .' and Masha

turns away.

'Well,' says Regina, 'commerce and slow accumulation – that's no good, it seems. Suppose we take a boat, and sail and roam, and find a shore. . . There's countries flat and full of dust. . . We'd plant a tree, and in its shade. . . Anywhere, we're sisters three.'

'No, no,' says Masha, 'the flatness and the dust – that's fine. It's us who are no good. Wrong attitudes. We have the wisdom. Wherever we go, whenever, there should only ever be an empty house, a tree. No landscape. A village – no fires, the smoke's a giveaway. No people that we have to kiss or kill. A crows' nest.'

'You girls,' Regina scolds, 'It's not like that at all. One thing follows another, I'm convinced of it.'

'And who convinces you, Regina,' Masha says, with a nasty edge. 'Ben? And if it's all a piece of string, there's an end. And – snip, snip – so, you can cut off lengths – and some are time in paradise, and some are time in hell. It all stops and starts again, Regina – it's not at all connected up.'

'At last!' says Delia. 'Some optimism! Like Furio says, 'Doctor Gritt's the world's best dealer!' An invention – it's what they used to call a miracle.'

The others laugh, and Masha spits for luck when Furio's name comes out.

'Maybe,' Regina says. 'We are observed. Always. Not by a spirit who cries in silence when we fall, would love to help us up. No, some watcher who steers, who makes a wake, a curve in the water that will disappear as we drive on, but the curve is beautiful to what it is that drives us to step this way or that – beautiful in mathematics, or some discipline we don't know what it is, besides, it's gone, it's all behind us, the water flattens out behind, it rises up ahead. We have to gaze ahead – the waves are vertical! Watch out! And we're designed, one of not many shapes . . . that watching, steering someone is scissors cutting a pattern from the paper us. . . Paper from reeds, dear Delia, pale flesh submitting to the sharpened edges that steer around the corners, cut and cut. . .'

'There must be music, Regina, if there's reeds,' says Delia.

'Oh yes,' Regina says. 'And when you've been cut out and fallen on the floor – maybe you get picked up, and they use you as a matrix, the paper overlays a cloth, and that too is cut out, falls on the floor but it is part of something – maybe a hanging, maybe a rope of silk from your first tree or . . . coronation robes or wedding garb. . .'

'The music, Regina,' Delia says.

'Oh, a dance with booted legs flung high, the sax family rootling up and down the steps, like it was Odessa, like it was Persepolis, Eliseum, a merry gopak: sirens. Sirens like they have on rocks, who mesmerise, and cop cars too: at the back, the merry devils, percussionists, tapping the boxwood blocks, the tinny cubes, the gourds. . . It's fun, Delia . . . you must join in,' Regina says. 'You have joined in.'

'And you think it's all connected up?' asks Delia.

'Yes,' Regina says. 'That's what I think. It goes on and on, because it has a structure, or we'd all fall off and end up somewhere else.'

'Have we got older?' Delia asks, worried. 'Is that an essential part?'

'No, we're just the same,' says Masha. 'We have less time left, though.'

'So it all matters less, looking back,' says Delia. 'It all gets smaller. Am I selling everything short, perhaps?'

'Time's up!' Regina shouts. 'What you don't know now, don't expect you ever will.'

*

'I can't stand them, my sisters,' Masha says. 'It's not important. You don't have to cling to them, and you can't abdicate. They were right to change the world, give it a shove, out of the rut where it was stuck, spare the poor horse from useless hammering. But everything's not so. Along that track – there's not just people trudging, who'll never have a horse and cart. They're hunted. Inedible, but game.'

'You can't help them – if you wanted to. Joining them – the last thing anyone would want . . . ' says the guy, next table.

'Wanting doesn't enter,' Masha says: 'It's that they're there, in the composition.'

'White telephones, a fine idea. I dialled you up, seeing you were spare. I'm Merry Duval, that's my name,' the guy on the phone says, winking over at her: 'Should you dance with me?'

'Is this trot a fox? or a turkey?' Masha asks, mischievously. 'You'd call the music "hot", that is for sure. I'm hot – are you? I was certain you would call me when I saw you at your table, with your lobster claw. So, is it true you're the richest person – in this hotel, at least?'

'Oh,' says Duval, 'I'm not rich. Wealthy, I'd say. Powerful's better.'

'These telephones – it's all nostalgia,' Masha says. 'They make you think of prostitutes. Me – I'm good, so it makes me think of *té dansant* – seeing you, a lobster quadrille, perhaps.'

'Might I sit close to you?' Duval asks with extreme courtesy.

'Of course, I'm waiting for some friends. Or sisters,' Masha says. 'Sit here. Or maybe you've a room?'

'Oh no,' Duval says. 'I lodge elsewhere. You get fresh crabs here, so. . .'

They do their business in a corridor.

'See,' Duval says, taking a knobbly figurine from his pants. 'This is a golden Hercules. I can't sell it on, or they'll think I pillaged it. You do it, and they'll know you did. Smile nice, they'll swallow their concerns.'

'It's very small,' says Masha. 'The club – looks like a baseball bat.'

Duval says, 'Well, do your best. As a baby, He was plump. It's mass He got, and growing quite elderly, what He lost.'

*

The fence – the expert trader – says, 'Wow! This again? Beneath, it isn't even lead.'

'I don't have my moral push behind the deal,' says Masha, giving up.

There is no deal.

*

'Well,' says Duval, 'Merry's my name, my nature is persistent. Next time, we'll try with Psyche. In my flight through life – my palette stays the same: pink and white, a yellow underside to clouds, a brush that's but a single hair, sometimes it hovers, hums, flicks a long tongue, takes sugar, and moves on. . . The panel, Masha, canvas – leave it black or white: don't stir the flesh, my dear.'

'I don't do sex,' says Masha, 'but I need cash. Is that a puzzle, do you think?'

'Oh, in my way, I'm a philosopher,' says Duval. 'And have there ever been unhappy philosophers? The cash? What must we do to have enough? A roof, some health. . . Is that so difficult? Is that philosophy, is that what supreme intelligence thinks is good?'

'Dance,' says Masha, 'you need. Sometimes a horse and cart.'

'Maybe your finger back,' Duval says, 'to give precision. Direction. And while we chat – why should I, having my wealth and artefacts . . . everything . . . still I call you at your table. . . ? No philosopher would do as much – hooking a single person with a name and sisters, it wouldn't fit the grander plan! Is there a plan? What we find, the plan – maybe it's us who made it anyway, right at the start! I was born a philosopher, Masha – were you?'

'Your name, Duval,' says Masha, 'it isn't yours – I remember seeing it, high on a wall. . .'

'And would a name, original, delight?' Duval asks. 'You find a name, never used before . . . is there some chrism there? Or if I'm called Redeemer, or Avenger – do you follow me, or do you flee?'

'You're not a philosopher of that sort,' says Masha. 'I hope you don't end with a single sentence, unequivocal, banal.'

'I have to rein in,' Duval says. 'If I foresee too much, I'd end up burning on the beach . . . A tar-barrel, Masha. That teaches better than a slate. The teacher tells you how to avoid a fate, not be too smart. . .'

'You make my head buzz with your questions,' Masha says. 'Must I have answers to them all?'

'Oh, I have all the answers,' Duval says. 'Otherwise, why ask the questions? Just to be a nuisance, Masha?'

'Tell me, Duval,' she asks, 'Something belongs to me – do I belong to something?'

'My name?' he asks. 'Does that belong? When I'm in Turkey, doing deals – of course I have another one. You don't have much, dear Masha – even your sisters are not yours. And you belong to whoever comes along. Or whatever comes . . . they used to say, that in the midst of death . . . we lie in wait. We're on an elastic thread, you see, everything is doubled up – coming and going all at once. You're thrown over some massive shoulder like spilt salt – I see you're not the superstitious type, but other are. They learn their lessons from your awful fate. Nothing is ever like it was – nothing is ever like it is, it's time, you see. You think it's rigid, like a watch. It's accidental. It's a tank that runs along with drivers quite unsighted, knocking down mosques and crushing fine Egyptian cats. . . On, on – black smoke and tireless tracks. Everything it hits – is accident. . .'

'I guess you get your stuff from the jihadis. . .' Masha says.

'Maybe they don't think much of me,' says Duval, 'But we do trades. I'm not the exalted type – a family and paradise and being good – those are the things I most avoid in life. Empires? That's juggling ice cubes in the sun. . .'

'I'm not much use to you,' says Masha. 'I'm glad.'

'Manuscripts,' Duval says: 'That's what comes next. Unread for centuries. People pay for wisdom. Has it been much use to you, Masha? People think it comes from experience – that's a prime mistake in philosophical thought, you know.'

'It ended bad for Ben,' says Masha. 'He'd have done

better as a Brother Charlie. Delia – a follower: she'd have read stuff till she died. Regina – surviving the batterings, that was her forte. She could have ducked. You're right, Duval – wisdom was perhaps their goal – but in the end, someone off the stage shoots the seagull, and the curtain falls. Is that where we get wisdom? As we shuffle out into the rain?'

'Hmm, yes, probably,' says Duval, pressing along: 'Your odd friends. . . ! Do the trees enjoy the air? Having their leaves mussed up? They bend, dance a cachucha, you watch their arms, but not their solemn feet pegged in. . . Then, the tempest. They surrender, up go their hands . . . and no one cares. Firewood! Or – there's the wildfire – they're firewood on the spot. You run. You've always known exactly when to run, dear Masha. That's your wisdom – no roots!'

'My trees were a platform,' Masha says. 'They let me see more trees.'

'Jihadis don't have a handle on it, nature,' says Duval. 'Living in the sand – it makes you cynical about all that. Now, Masha, I need you to say what's in the pages – medicine or maths. . . Those poems that say that what you see is lost for ever as you turn to write it down, and that too, at once is shelved and lost for ever. . . Oh no! I'm crying! How can that be? And now it's passed!'

He wipes his pale blue eyes, and smiles at Masha. 'There's manuscripts. Fragments, books all broken. I preserve it all, I need an indication, a pointer, to what they are. There's buyers everywhere – just be very, very careful, what you say, and what you sell. It's all that's left, and off it flies . . . never to make sense again.'

'I had in mind,' says Masha, 'something more exciting for my life – much, much more. And more significant. Collectors, autopsies – digging in those man-shaped holes. . . I'm not enthused, Duval.'

'I'm disappointed, Masha,' says Duval, not at all cast down. 'A civilisation – it's a tree. It grows, it gets chopped down. It's rotten, too tall, just in the way. Another grows – it's best not to attach: – you're right.'

'Oh no,' says Masha, 'I was attached. We all were. There's such variety! And such protection. They don't ask your name, but you can climb them, high as you like. The best thing is – there's forests. Infinity.'

'Paper,' says Duval. 'No more than that.'

'That's gone, Duval,' says Masha. 'Past. Leave it.'

'I know all that,' Duval says. 'It's not the past I sell. Cash only works right now. The present, Masha. That's where the danger lies.'

'So much?' asks Masha. 'We're talking so much cash it can do anything?'

'Oh, much, much more than what we give those guys,' Duval says. 'We know its value, Masha, the value of the cash. And it's calligraphy I'm in, not killing one another: where's the harm?'

'It sounds banal, that's all, Duval,' says Masha.

'These guys are all *ummi*,' says Duval. 'They don't read, they listen. What's this parchment say?'

'I don't read Kufi,' Masha says. 'Besides, it's been cut in half – it has no significance.'

'Of course, I have competitors,' disappointed, Duval says. 'My other halves . . . have other halves. It looks like walls of broken bricks stacked up; but in a frame, the right decor. . .'

'This one's a picture of the planet Mercury, shown as an old, old man,' says Masha. 'What's it worth?'

'Well,' Duval says, 'an old old man? Not much. But if it's cosmic, then of course. . .'

'I remember a book I read,' says Masha. 'It began, "At daybreak, my face still turned to the wall. . ." The guy thought he knew the weather. That's not exceptional at all.'

'"*Eh bien, mon Prince. . .*"' Duval, not to be outclassed, says, laughing. 'We all had founding books. . .'

That's another shared experience – both had a childhood, some traditions on the shelf.

'I'm not convinced. . .' says Masha. 'It's just trade.'

'Don't be too snobbish, dear,' Duval says. 'Your flesh is worth less by the kilo than these goatskins by the gramme. And where they come from – there's no nature left. None at all. There's only poetry. How sad. How profitable, if you know the business.'

'This is Bactrian,' Masha says. 'Something about cherries, cherry trees.'

'These bombardments,' says Duval. 'Better than archaeology. Throws the stuff up. Then they make a crater, deeper still. Copper. Lapis. . . The virgin's robes are lapis, but with your name, you'd know all that. . . It all gets tumbled round. Robes . . . virgins . . . no one wants to know about all that!'

'I only recognise what's figurative,' says Masha. 'You know there were people then, who looked like me.'

'That's sentimental,' Duval says. 'Those arabesques – they are the loops made by the butterflies – it's all done by algorithms – those look like us. They'll have our features on a screen somewhere, and when we board a boat, they'll search our bags. . . They recognise you by the maths.'

He holds up a head. 'They say it's Greek, but Greeks are febrile. This is the holy man himself, relaxed. . . The Greeks don't smile – this one – patience? Indifference?

Dreaming?'

'Falling asleep,' says Masha. 'We all look the same that way.'

'Some bare their teeth,' Duval says. 'The dreams. They say they're other worlds. That's nonsense. They are ours – we belong to those like our own does not belong to us. They're what you see when you are a fly, a penis, or a dingo dog. Not memories of what you were, memories of what you'll be.'

'How much?' asks Masha. 'The poem thrown in free.'

'It'll end with someone who'll want a body for the head – then sells it on,' Duval says. 'You mustn't think of that. We talk of coin – but really, we are ferryman. Poling the cadavers – do we really want the obols, on the eyes, prised from the mouth? A mucky deal, that. What do we spend them on? Breath fresheners? We're painters, Masha – we suck the lymph from what we sell – then it's dead fish, off they go for someone's feast. Bloodless. No tears, Masha.'

'No,' Masha says: 'I don't cry. You do, but you're a mountebank. You cry, just brine – I can do somersaults. . .'

And she cartwheels down the dune. Tears are one thing – that's the physiology: crying – you have to mean that, it's the vision, not just a name shuffled in among the rest you hope you won't be noticed, some smartass thinking they can spot your origins, if you think the earth is round or conical. . .

'And look!' shouts Masha – I'm spinning, not just down – I'm a wheel, I go round but up hills too. Everywhere. I'm the earth, the earth's a wheel, and if you're on the edge, you turn a thousand times faster than the hub. . .'

'That's it, Masha. 'Duval says. 'Guys want to be on the hub, they think that's the secret of the turn. No! Better the rim, in the oxshit and the daisies, faster and faster. . . That's where I want to be. . . It's where we both are.'

'Are you sure that's where I want to be?' asks Masha? 'The trees. . .'

'Oh, that's all past,' Duval says. 'Everyone's a soldier now – some, of course, are prisoners. Soldiers know two kinds of tree – the pine, the bushy top. You need the pine to aim with. Bushy tops are first to go, but now – all Gone! Wheels, that's what an army needs. That's what you are, Masha.'

'Oh, my poor sisters,' Masha thinks. 'When they raise the glass, the bottle – then the spotter draws his bead, his eagle eye . . . down they go, red wine all over, ruins the grass.'

'The Persians were great boozers,' Duval says, rushing along. 'They say they got it off Alexander, but whenever two or three sat down together – there it was, a wholesome red, I'd guess. Copying. That was the snag. They never did the variations, had a conversation – someone long before had set the stories down, the characters. Wine. "Today, space is resplendent, let's ride off on wine, to a fairy heaven – divine. . . No bit, no spurs, no bridle. . ." Silent forces, Masha. . . Drink – and out of the flask they come. . . Layla, Majnun, the rest. . . Do nothing, don't resist, be as idle as you can. . . On, on. . . !' He waves his arms. 'Of course,' he says, 'I'm not a fatalist. Getting where you want to go – it matters, otherwise, you wouldn't bother.'

'Can we really go so fast?' asks Masha. 'Mostly, things swoop and eat. A skydive – then you do it all again. Five times a day. Some by swoop and some by stealth. But, Duval, it's eats. All the rest's aesthetics.'

'Not the eats,' says Duval. 'The drinks. There must be a secret, because it's forbidden.'

'Sex,' says Masha. 'Lots of that's forbidden here and there. But there's no secret.'

'It's true,' says Duval sadly. 'The mystery is, people think that there's a secret.'

*

'Look,' says Duval. 'A silver anklet. Why don't you wear it, Masha. It's off a lakshi, a spirit of the trees,' and he presses it into her hand.

'This bells the cat?' asks Masha, laughing. 'Those tiny bells would scare the birds. . . And is it valuable?'

'Oh, the guy I got it off,' says Duval innocently. 'He didn't know its age. Though why that makes a difference . . . I suppose it's the illusion that if something lasts, then everything must do – or has a chance. Maybe they're right – the cities here – once, they were sophisticated, the most cultured in the world: museums of odd practices, but free! Crap governments – but people cocked a snook! You don't see snooks, cocked or not, around today. One day, my dear, it will all be put together. It always is. The problem's not in connecting – that's done in your head; but standing up the walls again . . . the roofs, the spires and minarets . . . Of course, the cities, they'll all need relocating somewhere else – the ground here's poisoned – in winter you can fry an egg on every pavement if your chicken is prolific. . . It shows who wins, of course, but who needs more dystopias? Those too are built inside your head. . .'

'I'm not sure about the anklet,' Masha says. 'Maybe you could give it back. . .'

'There's cops and soldiers everywhere, and other

operatives, each day is playing hopscotch on the powers,' he says. 'That guy? He's not a competition any more. . . I am a scholar, you're my consultant for the written stuff. He's just a trader – he's gone. Off the marketplace.'

'I know, Duval,' says Masha. 'Trading's no fun unless it's with forbidden stuff. But – that guy? Where'll he end up? You didn't pay him – so you sneaked? Gave his name to nameless ones? Said he was an emissary of the unnameable?'

'Oh, ending is the best thing that can happen to that creep,' Duval says. 'It's what occurs before that makes your teeth cry out.'

'What you do to him – someone might do to you,' says Masha, jingling her bells.

'Oh no!' says Duval, much put out, alarmed. 'How can you think that of your fellows? Vendetta? Tit for all the tat we sell? All these sides are warring, sure, but for much bigger things than you and I. Besides, it's always worked before. You have to spy, dear Masha, and betray: that is the secret of our trade.'

'I know,' says Masha. 'In the end, everything is trade and taxes. That's where sophistication's born. . .'

'Exactly so,' says Duval. 'Don't scare the birds when you are in your tree – mum's the word, and you'll find a nest, an egg for all your kids. . .'

'Oh no, Duval,' says Masha. 'Children is out. What if they grow like you and me?'

'An admirable modesty,' says Duval. 'If you aren't smart, you don't survive – that's what you tell them, the first time you take them into the forest, the darkness of the trees. . .'

*

Borders. You must know them well. They can drive through your village – or disappear overnight. Be careful – names stick, they follow you, they are your smell. That's what dogs are after, sniffing you. Many, like Masha, changed their name – that way, you get a whole new literature, new sisters too. Call yourself for those who occupy, those who bomb the others, or bomb you. You can't escape, though you can be a curiosity, and only when we're dead do we all become John Doe, or Jane. The perfect couple, they.

*

Duval has lockups: 'This stuff,' Duval says. 'The walls and bangles, body parts and ivories – will never be put back. Not together – that, they weren't ever. But one on top of t'other. When it's collected – you know that's gone for good. With luck – our good. The Gandharan stuff attracts the lay. . . Simple faith – when it's handed to the foot soldiers, you know there's someone big who tells them what to do. They'd sooner sit on roundabouts, cuddling their kids, seducing someone else's. No, Masha, it's all flat, and when the foundations get dug out – you know it's ready for a build.'

'We don't want that,' says Masha. 'I'm your partner, Merry. You're not in the building trade – you speculate on portable things. . .'

'Oh yes,' Duval laughs. 'That inexhaustible energy Gritt made – was a gift to everyone. No hods on ladders for us two! Mud bricks and wattle will do fine for everywhere. No, Masha, for me, it's not the cash – it's being right. Riding history like it was that bucking bull in blingy bars. . .'

'Being a seer,' says Masha, terrified, 'You're burnt! A barrel on the sands, you said!'

'Only if you blurt it out!' Duval says. 'Or if you've customers like Doctor Gritt, who'd pay to have you tip the hands. . . What else is there? Up your tree, dear Masha, with your sisters – cooking the pills? Yes, it's la dolce vita – in a silent mode. But – we know – trade and taxation. Those are the sun and snow, the rain, the dust, the horseshit that you need to make things grow. What religion or what self improvement comes on next – painted like Peking opera stars, or floured and farded like the ghosts – we must perch high, Masha. Watch everything, the all-seeing eye. We're packaging the past. We invent those civilisations that's been banged to dust. We can invent a deer park, the garden of delights – the silken roads, the gold pagodas, happiness lost and there . . . flittering among the trees it maybe is, or not. . .'

'It's decadent,' says Masha. 'We concoct the past, we are the messenger, the prophets . . . here the chisel, there the laws. . . And we stand back. "Now, get on with it," we say. . .'

'Yes!' says Duval, 'that's exactly it. They'll do it anyway, do what suits, whether they think their brains are wired or if their priests can read the turkey guts. Then – we get on with what we want to do!'

'The tree!' shouts Masha. 'The tallest I can find.'

'Oh Masha,' says Duval, 'that's what I feared. You are banal! Sit in your heaven? Watch the scurrying below? But – who will fill your basket? There's no ravens left – help from above is out. You need some groundlings to assist: to bring on the Corvo and the Canonau. *Le vin du souvenir.* Figs in and out of season – three kinds at least. There can be no sneaking down at night – the stores are always open, but there's guards and cameras that watch and light you up. You're a star – a hostage on screens around the universe.'

'I'll read the stuff I can,' says Masha, 'but there isn't much. It's whispers, and the relics – from all over – to China, down to Surabaya.'

'It's so,' Duval says. 'It's all stripped – a great clearout. "Everything must go", closing down: for cash. I know it all, Masha: I know everything – where it comes from, who brings it, where the money goes. My pile – it grows and grows. I'm the Genghiz with the money. If I wanted to. . .'

'If I were you,' says Masha, 'I wouldn't. I spied too – but close up. Not continental. I saw the poor and stupid pressed to do the dirty business.'

Duval waves his hands. 'You want to be my partner, so you are. Like it or not. You know as much as me. The risk is shared – it always is.'

'Everybody knows,' says Masha. 'It doesn't count. Spying only works for little things. Details. This museum's full of huge scenes – they're hung so everybody sees. They're only pictures. Nothing to fear, unless you jiggle them, they fall . . . the wall behind's exposed. . .'

'Here's a *qumqum* from Syria,' Duval says, holding it

up by its neck. 'There's one similar in New York. Forget the white telephones – we might be drinking *kumis*, you and I, punning on exotic foods. . .'

'As I said, Duval,' Masha tells him. 'Don't be drawn in. It's only pictures.'

'"The Lord said – I shall fill everywhere with ruins" – remember, Masha – don't take holy books lightly,' Duval says, laughing.

'Oh I've been reading worse than that,' says Masha. 'But it doesn't even brush against what's true.'

'My knowledge, Masha,' Duval says. 'I could pull every string. That's what the creation's made of – string.'

'You're wrong, Duval,' says Masha. 'Whatever is the tool you need – it isn't knowing stuff, or cash. Lots of people have those. . .'

'Fiddle, Masha,' Duval says. 'One of these lockups – it is packed with cash. Then there's my head, well-stocked – you've no idea – my contacts, knowing the inside of everything. . .'

*

'See what's in this sack,' Duval says. 'They say it's golden pheasants. Do the assay. . .'

'They've little crowns,' says Masha, peeking in. 'And

ducktails. Like those haircuts people had. Maybe they're geese, or hybrids, semurghs, maybe. . .'

'Look them up,' says Duval, quite offhand.

'They walk!' says Masha. And they do.

'Oh no!' shouts Duval. 'Are they a warning? Or an auspice? Check the reference, Masha, quick – no one here keeps birds – they've all been eaten when they ate the grain. . . Find what they are – decapitate them quick, you'll find a tulwar . . . .'

'Absolutely not,' says Masha, setting the pair down. They wander off, there's a little stand of sunflowers, they go in among the stems. . .

'It's a message, that's for certain,' Duval says, much agitated.

'So,' Masha says, 'you must know what it means, who sent them, all of that.'

'Knowledge is a sabre,' Duval says. 'You only use it when you ride a feisty horse that takes you out of range. . . Two geese . . . mates, you and I . . . two turkeys – sitting ducks. Swans or peacocks – that would be class. . .'

'They're never peacocks,' Masha says. 'Not with those tails. They'd have usurped – they've little crowns.'

'They could be swans, singing the last song,' says Duval, testing the padlocks on the sheds. 'Those kinds of bird – don't live in trees. Maybe that means you're not the target, Masha. . .'

'I read,' says Masha. 'Interpretation is your task.'

'They're falcons,' Duval says. 'Not crowns – crests. Spitcurls.'

'They can't be,' Masha says. 'They waddle.'

'They've found their prey,' Duval says. 'They drop out of character.'

'We groan under these empires,' Masha says. 'Until our eyesdown metalwork finds us a space. But when they fall, until the next one takes its place – there's omens, threats, vendettas from all sides. And if you write things down – watch out!'

'That doesn't comfort,' Duval says. 'Those occidentals thought they could sit at home and press a key and buzz off some stinging craft to zap offenders and their friends. It isn't so . . . we know, you need be on the spot, and pay your rents. Trade and taxation, Masha, without those, there's no repression, no hegemonic class. . .'

'Fine words, Duval,' says Masha. 'What do we do? The trees are all knocked down. There is no "up". The flowers – follow the sun, like dogs on a leash. Where does it all go, Duval. . . ?'

'The sun? Goes round and round,' Duval says, packing gold into a sack. 'That's what I – we – mustn't do.'

The sun burns them where they stand, two mud bricks: at odds with how the hand has fallen, how the entrails squirm, what quarter of the winds. . .

'It's like Delphi,' Duval says. 'The seer takes smoke – then, breathing out, it all coils round. You can't see fuck all. Shadows. Neurons sparking in your brain. The bright eternal tunnel that means you'll journey ten seconds more – then . . . it's up to relatives, lawyers, what becomes of you, your skinsack, last words invented, carpenters and worms – on the alert. Good luck!' And he weeps.

'Relatives? Lawyers? I'm amazed,' says Masha. 'You have all those?'

'No, not even those black birds that rend and flap,' says Duval, weeping more. 'You have your sisters, Masha. Alina waiting where they wait – that room stuffed full with strangers wearing ancient clothes. Forever, Masha – there's no trains, not for eternity. . . Delia with that irritating smile, Regina. . . Oh no! Ben – burnt up, like spawn sundried out in ponds. . . Those inventions all aborts. . .' Duval lies in the dust, spreadeagled with grief for himself.

Masha punches him – all she can find's the back of his head. 'You appropriated me,' she shouts. 'My life! Memories. People.'

'You didn't cling to them,' Duval says. 'They suit me well. Forget your sect that no-one's heard of, forget the community you didn't like, and lost . . . the feasts the rituals. . . You're not-new Soviet woman who's renounced all that and has to read about yourself in books. . . Your surface, Masha, is quite slippery. Things tumble off you on the floor. . . No parents, no cat or dog, no crazes and no loyalties. . . I pick the pieces off you, like picking cherries off a plate. A plastic vessel, not like these here, in the lockups, that people pay a patrimony for and never use. We all have a glass case, Masha, where we stack our precious things. You don't. You can expect to lose that stash of staples in the charity bag they handed you. . .'

'If you run, Duval,' says Masha, 'take me with you, if you run alone. I'm your disciple – from you I've learned my spirituality – and if they take you, leave the key for the lockup were the money is.'

'I'll brush up my martial arts,' says Duval. 'That's spirituality and kicks together.'

'Challenge them!' says Masha. 'Maybe if you win, they'll let you go.'

'The woods are dark,' Duval says. 'Defence is what's required. It's in the head. The feet have their restrictions. . . '

*

Masha never finds the lockup with the cash. The other sheds are full of painted dust and cataracted glass, the water pots have come unrivetted. Restoration will see it right.

Duval has disappeared – in Masha's imagination, he is safe. It's not the safest place to be, but he has room to walk about, try different strategies.

'Masha,' Masha's imagination says, 'you could ask around, find out where he is. He has the key. . .'

'No,' Masha tells her imagination. 'If he's around to gather luck, he'll be alive, maybe outside. If not, he'll be inside. If it's very good – I'll find the cash, and that will be all of that. I'll have new life, Duval – his destiny.'

Philosophy, if you dig deep down – says it ought to matter who gets hold of you – the faithful or the democrats, the pragmatists, essentialists. . . But – day to day, it's much the same – the food where you've ended up, is different, if there's any, but there's never food enough. Interrogations: it depends how it may go if someone's read a book on brains. No one believes you have a secret, or that anything you think has some significance, but Duval loves questions because he loves his answers.

It may pall, of course, the room, the guys, the wasted time, the waste.

*

Duval packed his goods in carpets. Masha sleeps, rolled in a fine Tabriz. A stirring – from close by – that's a Shiraz.

'Hey,' says Auric. 'Duval let me doss down here.' It isn't likely. What can you say?

'Duval – he won't be extinguished,' Auric says. 'Who could put him out – that guy. . .'

Masha can't conclude the thought: she asks the guy his name.

'We're units,' Auric says. 'They count us, goddam positivists – and use the sum to justify. Bombs, charity, kindhearts and bigots – the more you are . . . the more you can attract. Because our stuff – we do it in the road – is drab, insistent, we seem less worthy than the well-shod guys, in an office, smelling good. All these experiences – I know you're Masha, Masha – Duval chose you for your mutilation, that way you couldn't point him out. That should endow you with a moral thrust. It can make you great, memorable, at least. You're a living lesson, Masha. Uplift. The struggle for the good. A problem though, there is: an incoherence – you avoided that great benefactor – Doctor Gritt. Free energy for ever. You ran out on him, his squad. . .'

'I saw my path,' says Masha. '"Leave" I heard. Then – there were leaves. . .'

'A charge,' Auric repeats. 'That's what they look for – *prises de positions*. Celebrating what is – the basic goodness in us all that takes a pick to prise it out. . . And then – the folly and the greed – you must cast on those your critical glance. . . Your example will spring forth – maybe better if you're quite well-known, discreetly wealthy, battling with obscure disease, and so and so – your example will raise us for the day. Your suffering, Masha – has the power to make you great, a sage. . . You won't need to write a word – that's all been said and writ.'

'I know,' says Masha. 'And I am all of that. In my imagination, Auric. I don't need your puff, nor sisters treacherous and viperous, no white telephones and pickups in nostalgia bars, no muddling through. . .'

'Exactly so,' says Auric. 'You agree with everything I've said. We're a great pair.'

'Maybe so,' says Masha. 'No touching now. You're beetly and a chancer. But you'll do.'

'Duval,' says Auric, ignoring her. 'Knew too many people. That's a trap. He was too generous. Financing everyone – you only do that after you're an emperor.'

'You don't get to be an emperor without ambition. Duval had that,' says Masha. 'That meant he couldn't stop. Maybe they'll let him out – his story isn't interesting outside himself. . .'

'All this stuff,' says Auric, pointing down the line of sheds. 'You couldn't make a civilisation from it – but it does give lustre to your own. Shows you're in the stream, that you've respect. It shows your female side. Me – I'm a musician – that's what it means, to do it in the road. The acoustic's cruel. It's the devil. Not that you need summon Him – He's on your back.'

'Duval – all he had was relics,' Masha says.

'Oh, he had cash too,' says Auric. 'He had the weight, the friends. . . On, on, you rush – it's coronation. Maybe you want, instead – one of my songs. "Arise: ye prisoners. . . !" Could be he's one of them . . . right now. That gives it extra strength.'

'It's not my thing,' says Masha. 'The devil's dance. I'm for the prisoners, of course.'

'We should bear in mind the probability of flight,' says Auric.

'Suppose Duval said my name?' says Masha. 'And in a context?'

'That's an egg,' says Auric. 'You could wait to see

what's in it. . .'

'No,' Masha says. 'We'll run. There's *maquis, macchia,* here – you can't run through it, birch trees you can – those, the legs of white foals, they say. Here, everything is boiled and stewed. The pines – Roman, but salty from the sea, the bark peeling off like velvet from deer's antlers . . . the rocks – ruins of houses never built. . . Auric! You can't run here, it's all up. . . ! Fractured and undergrown, herbs, burrows, samphires perhaps. . .'

'I hate journeys and explorations,' Auric says, trotting alongside: maybe he hums a chorus from that opera, 'The Forests of Lithuania': into his eyes there come the nests of slumbering asps, the lizards yellow and green, miraculous *gecki* on the vertical.

'Our relics,' Masha says. 'Dead souls, no one needs them. Dust.' She sees the bands of people crossing, criss-crossing, crosses and crescents, dropping their bundles, cutting a door-frame, mourning a pony. . . Imagination all. . . a marvel.

'Mind the traffic!' Auric shouts.

'I can't see it,' Masha says. 'I'm the traffic anyway.'

'Where are we going, where did we come from?' Auric chants.

'The fire!' shouts Masha. 'We forgot the fire! Set Duval's flame to all his stuff – fuse it, make it a globe, a glob of vitreous frit. The row of sheds, the pious images, unrhyming verses, pans and skillets, silk mantles, wool from the Karakum, shards and forbidden instruments – all together – up in an orange conflagration – the unread books that ground our wisdom, articles of faith, derision and despair – burn it all. We can't make anything new from all that stuff. . .'

'New, Masha?' Auric asks, quite breathless, bleeding from the stings and thorns – 'What's new for you? I'm tied into my modes – and you're bound down, gigantic, tethered . . . your sisters and your booze, your sacrifice that no one wants – there's nothing new, just fiddled variations. . . Duval's pretensions, the salvage, ceramics lined in galleries for uncomprehending gawps, the installations that travesty dead potters' kilns. . . Vanity, oh vanity, dear Masha! Bury the sisters, and here they come again, fresh ones with kids that stick like burrs. . . No rest, no glory. . . In this scrub – it is impossible to run . . . you reach the highway, then there are cleared lots for tented camps. . . The new! Its baggy skin, the rocking teeth, tongue cherry-red with some affliction, the cod-eyes, lids that don't quite close, the dusty hair like thyme gone wild. . . Burn all that you see, a hecatomb of unpaid rents, ailments uncured – that is your new, poor Masha; demented memory, fixed on the primal shack up in the trees, your unrelated sisters chattering, and swinging by their tails. Terrible, Masha. And Doctor Gritt who's made the energy spin on out for ever! The problem's solved, the second law that runs the system down – repealed! Steady state, Masha! You ran from that – where are you running now? Around you'll go, and end up here. . .'

'All that is so, poor Auric,' Masha says. 'At least here we aren't in jail and putting Xs on the wall with blood and pus.'

'Not so fast, Masha,' Auric says. 'A life that's not contained the Everything – is incomplete. I don't say worthless – but there's still cards face down, a die tipped on an edge and frozen. You must have renunciation, ecstasy, persecution, vainglory, rhetoric, caress . . . wildfire and tidal waves. . . Everything, Masha – falling off the tree – falling on grass, love and crawl, the true the false . . . The worst – is consistency, following the book, the rule, the good, the faith – the tidbit of reward, tomorrow, for eternity . . . self-satisfaction, Masha – that is death in life. . .'

'Yes, yes,' Masha says, 'I see all that. That's what a musician's life imparts – I've had all that myself. What now?'

'Don't be sad, Masha,' Auric says. 'There's nothing more. Do everything, and then – there is no more. Logic,

Masha. Science. Those are the full stops. We're all King Roger – first the scarlet cloak, a kingdom bestowed on you, you alone, by God – and then the monastery, the trembling, sickness, the scourge, the mouldy bread. . .'

On he talks, his words a carpet of live flowers. . .

They haven't set the sheds on fire. They haven't seen the guys in the plump white cars they use round here. . . Until . . . they do!

'This time,' shouts Auric, 'no questions! Into the trees and up the scarp!'

'Wait!' says Masha. 'Those guys – may not be after me. . . It could be you, Auric. You've seen it all. . . It could be your time is up.'

'It all depends,' says Auric, 'on the colour of the eyes – this century at least. Duval – was a blue-eyed Turk, fresh off the steppe. The next Master, a new generation, sticking everything together with runny glue. . . Your eyes, Masha – like apricots. Just hanging in your face. Waiting to be picked, ripened or premature. . .'

'It's true,' says Masha. 'I've had sisters. Humanity's too heavy round my neck. I'm edible, like a sheep, starting with my orange eyes. But – who would want the life of Doctor Gritt – or of Duval? No one would, though both were Masters. I'm the bright Slave, who sees, survives. . .'

'You're wrong,' says Auric. 'Slaves survive where Masters don't because there's millions of them. It isn't you who wins the pot, dear Masha – it's your lookalike, semblable, frère.'

'Oh no!' says Masha. 'A brother! That would spoil it all! I need to be a lioness, autonomous, not a footsoldier in a troop of apes.'

'We'll talk it through,' says Auric, as the guys come close. 'When we've escaped.'

*

They're up the slope, into a suburb, a huddle of pastelled bungalows . . . maybe a favela. Up the hill. . . Many stares. . . There's even steps, banks to keep the gardens in – up, up they go, past the bleary vipers, bees red and black, ants black and red, birds grounded and birds dead.

The guys, in their brown suits and co-respondents' shoes – did they come to bring encomia? Or restraining tape? They'll never know, Masha and Auric. What matters is – they're at the top. Time for Masha to see the colour of Auric's eyes. Not blue, for sure.

*

'THE PLAIN OF PENITENCE', Auric reads from the plaque.

'It's like Persepolis,' he says. Before them lies an expanse, rostra and columns with every design of capital. No Shah of Shahs, of course, but then, the show must go on, but not on and on.

He reads out to Masha: 'Praise, but especially blame. It's a conundrum. Apology. Remorse. Left to history, it's murky, a legalistic grey. Relativism abounds. Power rarely goes into the dock. A "sorry" always comes too late – that's by definition: no one apologises before the act. . . And – who cares? If apology's required, it's because the case is closed. So – the Plain was laid out for all – the tall poppies – to confess, apologise, have done.'

'It's for everyone,' says Auric. 'You gather here, and some guy who's done wrong – some chief, that is – apologises. Repents is optional. Living or dead, guilty, innocent, ignorant or well-informed – the populations come to see the scene. . . Then, the big guys, they tread the boards. So, you're shriven. Bring along your priest, your publicist. They're all there – your mates, those you wronged as well. It's sincere, for sure – everyone can see it, yea or nay. And then – we're done with it. That is the best. No one is reconciled, no justice done. . .'

'It's too late for Ben,' says Masha. 'He's not here – was justice done?'

'You haven't got the gist,' says Auric. 'Apart from being dead – I think his case is moot.'

'Delia and Regina – they'd be here. Someone has done them wrong, for sure,' says Masha.

'No, Masha,' Auric says. 'You're still not there. This is big stuff, not tipping relatives into a ravine. But – there is another take, my dear. My gain, my profit from neutrality. The music. Big bands, big systems. Work: for all of us. The Locals can rejoice. "Song of the Forests, Forests of Lithuania, Hansel and Gretel" . . . then there's the classics – "Woodman, woodman, spare that tree", the Woodchoppers' Ball. . .'

'Don't ingratiate,' says Masha. 'I know you know about my thing for trees. I come from where they are no more. They are my salvation. Penitence is good, for sure, but so is my security. I've no need to bleat out on the plain, nothing to feel contrition for. I am an innocent, alas. . .'

'We should have set the fire,' says Auric. 'Let nature have it back – our heap of artefacts . . . the cash we should have got. No lesson there, all mute, awaiting the embalmers, dead stock. . . People remember fires – the library at Alexandria, not its books unread. It is the flames, the fires – those stick and smoulder in the brain. And as for penitence – you lived with parrots, Masha: how they love the shiny things, beak everything to see if it is edible . . . we love a show! Without them, guys like me would starve – our saxes summon, squawk and lubricate. . .'

'Enough!' shouts Masha. 'We didn't cash it in! Our inventory. Forget it, now. Duval for sure is charged with crimes against the state – sale of the patrimony, mercification of the truth, the beauty – our striving ancestors traduced: their gewgaws and their pans – all at a discount. . . It's my regret, I never went into trees or parrots – their subjectivity, all that; still less the future. As for all the rest – that went into me, not me to it . . . the future too. Best not put the light, the knife on that.'

They skirt the central stage: there's floury faces rehearsing, mouthing, tearing floury wigs. 'Aeschylus,' says Auric. 'They never stop.'

'Duval was brilliant,' Masha says. 'The quips! The ambition – he knew no slippery foothold, he climbed the ladders, like a winged angel . . . but you, Auric, you're a mouthful of thorns. Moralistic, too.'

'Duval was destined for the top,' says Auric. 'Who knows – someone might even vote for him. Trust nature – it must feed us, they used to say . . . and so they bodged up empires, filled with slaves. Trust science, they said then: it poisoned us. Duval said – trust me! And no one did. Maybe though . . . we did, just we two. Too bad.

Now, Masha, you must start all over. Find someone to transport us somewhere else; we'll need to change our names for if we land . . . Mostly it's flat. Aim for flat green, not yellow, and not brown.'

'A balloon,' Masha says. 'That way there's no destination. All's natural. Trust the wind, the heat. If they shoot you down – where you land, that is your destiny.'

*

'Here's the basket,' Masha says. 'I'm never now without. And the envelope – best silk, taken from the Road – I don't believe the verses written on it – many do. Now, Auric – blow! It's physics. Arise, basket and bag! Auric! Blow!'

They rise. They see Everything, spread out below, and out of reach.

'Ballast!' says Masha. 'We forgot. Not me, I'm far too light. Who does that leave, dear Auric? We must lift, or else we tumble down. A sacrifice may be required. . . A destination too . . . over a sea, an ocean. . . ? Mouths waiting open . . . straight down, no throat . . . oh dear! Mongolia? – they'd welcome us for sure.'

'Each has their map,' says Auric, clinging on. 'For some, the green is Amazon, for others, it is alp. My map has countries yet to come, and others sketched out in my dreams. I have the fire inside, the fire we didn't set, so, we can drift, quite infinitely. My dragon's breath – is inexhaustible. . . There go the forests of Romania, quite desolate. . . Over there's the Don, Masha, much changed from when we read the books. . . Some places gone to powder, some at night glittering like mirrorglass or sequins. . . You are the captain, Masha, you decide. Earth or air? I am the fuel, the fire. . .' He puffs, he talks.

Everywhere looks much the same – 'That's an illusion,' Masha says. 'Some places welcome you like gods, your machine is noiseless – first it circles like a fly, then it descends – a dove, a vulture, then a boat with painted eyes, a garland for your neck, a basket full of eagles – we could end like Duval, leading an army of a million warriors, ten million horses as the entourage . . . in their sights sand, ever sand, and crumbling cities built of yellow mud. . . Or else – we'll end, like Duval – being tortured on a chair. . .'

'Masha,' shouts Auric. 'You must navigate!'

'There's the one thing that balloons can't do,' says Masha, 'and that is steer.'

*

They land, of course. Most everybody does. It must be science too – though science doesn't steer.

*

'We've been expecting you,' the guy says, 'though this guy with furrowed face. . .' and he pokes at Auric, 'wasn't on our menu. And you, my dear,' he peers at Masha, her sweat, her dust – 'we had in mind a beauty, decked out as if she was a Tlemcen bride in silks.'

'Oh,' Masha says, grasping that here, they are secessionists, 'my silk went into transport.'

'There's second life,' says the guy. 'Here's yours! You're lucky. Maybe you fell out the basket a first time. That's the myth, for superstitious folk. Now, we'll picture you again. Stand on these steps, as though you came by 'plane. New life! New you! These are our pics. Your stoker here,' he pushes Auric away. 'He doesn't figure – he goes over there. He can be your fan.'

Auric goes behind a line of cops: there's red, blue, yellow, green – bright poor enthusiasts, each keen to make a noise. Dressed loud.

'This is awful,' Auric says to Masha when the greeting's done. 'These guys want entry to their authentic selves – they've already taken ours. They'll brush some brocades on you, Masha – paint on an Infanta's dress.

They want to separate, secede, so's to be like everybody else: pumped up.'

'They changed the colour of my eyes, gave me big breasts,' says Masha. 'A speech to read. So far, so good – we'll make a final judgement when we see the eats. . .'

'Well,' says Auric, 'I won't do music for them. No marches, and no jigs. No forest chants, no roundelays. If we must be opportunists, I'll at least intrigue and plot.'

'Yes,' Masha says, 'dear Auric, you have an outlook that is quite malign. But – don't unsaddle me. You'd end up where I am. You may not find it enviable. We must be very, very careful here. They'll want to make a statue, me – a monster Hercules in gold: and take us round in open cars. Maybe you could drive. . . My head on coins, yours on a spike . . . it's like Petronius: the architecture is New Rome, but – who did they mistake me for?'

'Maybe there was no mistake,' says Auric. 'You are the clay. It's me they didn't titivate and knead. Quick – stow the balloon beneath my arm . . . it is our tunnel, the side gate unguarded, the sentinel made drunk. Our getaway. . .'

'It's another imaginary place,' says Masha, 'where we shan't feel at home, people will look askance. . . All countries are imaginary – here, this one's a new-born, just been dropped. . .'

‘Oh no,’ says Auric, ‘you’ll learn the accent and the dress. Talk straight, respect the myths. Remember, Masha, you’ve no folklore left. And when you worked with Doctor Gritt – that didn’t last. Then living up those trees – I even doubt that you believe in sisterhood. . .’

‘No, no,’ says Masha, ‘you’re wrong. There’s nothing negative in my life. It’s all a lesson, laid out like garden plants and herbs. . .’

‘Exactly so,’ says Auric, ‘nature – the great conservator – tradition with that fascist twitch. The furious spasm. . . All shoots up peacefully – then the whirligig’s unleashed, and everything is smashed, the bushes – macedonia: red fruit into gore. . . The hardy who survive – a tortoise and some worms. . .’

‘No, Auric,’ Masha says. ‘Nature is our ground, the bass. Our melodies, our discords – they depend on it. . .’

‘While we’re on this tack,’ says Auric, ‘let me tell you, Masha – nature isn’t real. It’s chaos. Random, Masha. Chance. It just acts very, very slow, follows meanders, designs eccentric, birds that cannot fly, fish that do, and breathe and walk. Quite unreliable. No rules, Masha, no logic – just instincts, customs, little processes. All arbitrary. Clytemnestra, Masha – she came from an egg! She hatched!’

‘So do we all, Auric,’ Masha says. ‘That shows how

you're wrong.'

*

'You haven't twigged,' says Auric, discomfited. 'There is no ground. Insects are blown from isle to isle on winds. . . rats borne on logs, cats in a suitcase . . . the virus in an aeroplane. . . The music wanders, from ear through to other ear . . . wind, Masha, wind. . .'

'I weep,' says Masha. 'It's right I do. It is the best we can.'

'Courage!' shouts Auric. 'They want you to be human here – a bride for sisters who can cosset and advise. Sincere and chaste – soothing and caring . . . potential mother, but not yet. . .'

'Do all the brothers want to bed me, then?' asks Masha, quite appalled.

'Oh no,' says Auric. 'They want a sister too. Soft and hard, mediating, leading. . . Weep when you send the soldiers off, and weep when they come hobbling back. . . You are the new, Masha: wear the old vestments, remember Mona Lisa – everybody loves that smile. . .'

'It seems to me,' says Masha, 'yours is the sweetest time. The first delight I've seen in here and now. Your role is best.'

'Of course,' says Auric, 'you're who's standing on the box. But – I'm doing trades with cynics round the back.'

*

'Look, Auric,' Masha says, 'Do we want all this? This show, this nascent country – it's a scenery. How did I even meet and trek with you? Carpet rolls, that's what we were in? My past – was searching for perfection. We stabilised the world – Gritt did. It's not his fault it totters. First, science was his garden – the treats all hidden 'neath the cucumbers – although at least you'd guess that they were there. Then – the perfect hand: you know it must exist, each pack of cards must hold it. That's maths. Gritt – the most logical of persons . . . first save the world, then creep in through its ear to see if somewhere there's a brain inside . . .

'There was poor Ben – his quest too – perfection: – juggling those imperfect players, lumpish philosophers, Lugers folded in their notepads – but still . . . a plan he had . . . .

'And now – forced landing. Do I want to stay. . . ?'

'I'm no friend of nature,' Auric says. 'No brothers, and no sisters. I can do without quite well . . . nurture or nature, it's the same to me . . . I'm easy – that's what "here and now" entails.'

‘If we duck out,’ says Masha, ‘They’ll think you were a spy, that you constrained or kidnapped me. To be frank, dear Auric, you’re not up to that. But – fear of my fate disturbs me. Dolled up, salute the gaudy flag, mouth mournful anthems, there go the guys on horses, guys in tanks . . . the dances, stamps and shuffles, the national epics you must learn – two thousand verses at the least, then there’s religion, and the tax . . . the national days with bars all closed, and then those mountain guys – want to secede, it seems they too have songs, a poet, national animal . . . horses and tanks again, dear Auric, and oh! – those whittled souvenirs. . .’

*

‘Look,’ Masha says, to the guy who greeted them. ‘Suppose I leave? Like Anna Garibaldi on her horse – except, from me, you’d keep the horse. . .’

‘Maybe you haven’t understood,’ says the guy, ‘You are our symbol.’

‘Oh,’ Masha says, ‘I’m full of symbols. But – messiahs come – and then they go. The founding father founds – he doesn’t build and decorate. The motherland – she doesn’t ripen and become a gran.’

‘It’s true,’ the guy says, thinking far ahead. ‘But you’d

need go off in your balloon. And maybe we would keep your mate, so's you don't come back.'

'That's fair,' says Masha, much relieved. 'And if I left behind a token – say, fraternity? Equality? My gift of symbols?'

'Don't think of it,' the guy says. 'That's been often done. There's turmoil, disappointment. Best only leave the enigmatic smile that everybody loves.'

'At least,' says Masha, 'if you do a statue, no one can break my index off. Think of Anna Garibaldi – that pointing finger's all you remember, up on her hill above the jail . . . on, on, her horse! Whither – only she knows. That's a good laugh! Where'd she hope to end? In Moscow?'

The guy doesn't follow – he says, 'None of these countries existed once. They all needed to be planted. Now – some are sequoias. Some are four-by-fours.'

'You're telling me!' says Masha. 'I'm part of deportations. Those often come in fashion.'

'I don't mind where you're going,' the guy says. 'So long as it's in the balloon.'

*

'I could rob you, Masha,' Auric says. 'I've done it

before. I'm not a mean type – but we picked each other up . . . really, we unrolled each other. It wasn't consonance we had.'

'You stole my Hercules,' Masha interrupts.

'It's ballast,' Auric says.

Masha hasn't thought of Auric like he is – what he says he is – a revelation. That someone so useful to her, so understanding too, should be exactly what he looks like – a sneaking thief. One you can't tell anyone about. And yet, apart from the fake statuette, unless they give her presents here, she has nothing he can steal.

'You've qualities abundant, Masha,' Auric says. 'Your trouble is – you have no plot. Me instead – I am all plot. Plot's what I do. I shan't stay here to guarantee you won't return . . .' and as he talks, he fits the basket to the silken cloud; they climb on board as though it were a boat escaping from the rhythm of the waves – up, up – and Auric's breath is sour and green, it fills the silk until they find a solid platform made of air, high above the country that is all imagination – 'Where are the eats?' asks Auric, in an unkindly way.

'There's eggs,' says Masha. 'Very lightly boiled.'

They crack them – inside, there's the green, yellow, red and blue of national parrots, snatching at each others' feathers, the shards of shells that stick – they tumble down, learning flight and gliding on the way. . .

'You cretin,' Auric shouts, and stands up tall, wavering on the basket edge and peeing on a city down below. 'We could have stayed at least a day and had a banquet, met some patriots, bankers who would pay to stop an insurrection. . .'

'Everybody's motivated by their values,' Masha says: 'The cops, the insurrectionaries – only you, poor Auric, you have a plot to ride that bounces you from fiddle into faddle. . .' On she talks. Should she push Auric off – and risk ascending – like the larks that go so high you hear them ever louder and they've become invisible. . . ? What is up there? Why is it blue – it should be black – no one comes back to talk of rocky cities on the other planets, maybe where the holy books have won the day. . . Maybe on Mercury they're chaste and faithful, or maybe they have a book that tells them No! – it's fruit machines and virtual friends the path to happiness . . . That's a puzzle for philosophy, one of its themes, you see it on TV. . . The curiosity, the doubt. . .

'I lack the courage,' Masha thinks, 'for salutary murder.'

She pulls Auric back inside, and they embrace – the space inside is meagre, and their fear is great.

'Whatever happens to me,' Masha says, 'I'm the same

everywhere. Only the places look all different.'

'That's solipsism,' Auric says, 'but you've nothing I could take. If I took your life – what would I do with it? Is it big or small? It's valuable to you alone – if we were peasants, I'd need find someone else to milk the goat. As it is – you're the pound of feathers in the air. We're modern, Masha, units in experiments, we can be counted, but we cannot hoe a row of beans, or shoot a wolf. You'd fall as fast as me, your brother. . .'

'No!' shouts Masha. 'That's not it at all. You're not my brother – if we fall, I'll spread my wings like Icarus – you're a pound of lead, poor Auric, or a bag of twiggy sticks. Where I'd land, I'd fertilise, or vanish as an orange flower, a spurt from a volcano's craw. . . The fall's the same – I told you, Auric, everywhere the fall's the same. It's architecture that distinguishes. . . That, and the colour of our eyes. . .'

'You may be right,' says Auric. 'How can I reply to that? You've nothing. We have nothing under us, and over us, but air. How strong it is, the air – holds us, speeds us like arrows . . . We're comrades so. . .'

'Another fallacy,' says Masha. '"Nothing is from nothing built. . ."'

They argue on. They have no chains, those can't be lost, nor used to lighten up their craft. . . And Auric's breath is weaker now, whatever holds them up is slackening –

'The sea! The sea!' shouts Auric. 'Not that! Oh no! Those fish, indifferent, the sponges, passive in your bath – out here they're eyes and belly, squids with beaks . . . ! Help us, dear Masha. Blow, and bring us to that rocky shore – there is no train to Leningrad, no Kreml' that awaits you; stop thinking there's another tale and other places unimagined – you have not escaped your destiny. It's true the plot may take a different twist – the seagulls here are real and hungry, there's no ploughman sees us drop like Icarus – so, blow, Masha, there's the cliffs, a rocky outcrop – inland, more sisters, probably. . .'

They land. Maybe they regret the country they had left, their being symbols, tiles upon a roof of state . . . the banquets and the equerries, watching the soldiers up and down, brass bands and cannons, war and peace, all that.

It is too late. They walk upon the land, there is no architecture – the breeze takes off the basket, the balloon flies on to rescue other stranded souls and no doubt strands them on some rock. . .

'I can handle Auric,' Masha thinks. 'He wants goods, not lives. He'll need a partner, maybe me, just as Duval did. And he's not kind – that's the worst, a hint of kindness, a touch – then savagery, intended, unintended, it ends all the same, goes on, the same.'

'Oh, it's not so bad,' says Auric. 'There's a village there, we can mingle with the tourists, tell a tale, they'll buy us drinks, be kind.'

'Yes,' Masha says. 'Someone's always kind. Everything has always been there, where it was and is. Everything always will be so, just so. Even if it all falls down, they'll brush the ruins off and tell us how it was. Every detail. Me – I'm the wanderer, the bee, the particle with shoes. I arrive, and then I go. How we see things, Auric, depends only on the color of our eyes. Everything is always there, before us on the road.'

'Come, Masha,' Auric says. 'Let's bum some drinks, and find a way to get back what we just gave up.'

'Is that it, Auric? Gardening? Candide, enjoying it, the weeds and all?' asks Masha.

'And who are you?' asks Auric. 'Have you a special insight, Masha, written in your walk-off part? A good guy, who hands out parcels, instead of taking them? Turn things around. Make it all different, and when you're safe, back in your tree – remember to let your basket down, and hope it's filled . . . by the good person, strolling by. . . '

'Fuck you, Auric,' Masha says. 'You let the basket drift away. . . And anyway – there's someone who'll have started it, the fight. The battle's never eye to eye – there's you and me. What starts it off – is politics. There's weakness on my part, perhaps, distraction, some excess: or – my place just being there – desirable, or on the way to somewhere else. There's starting, Auric, and there's going on and on. . .'

*

'Sing on, Masha, sing your aria, your air,' says Auric, losing patience. He works the tourists. 'See!' he says. 'New life!' He waves a brick of notes. 'It's like they say – the tale, and not the teller.

'They're generous – we're exiles – tall poppies, scythed down. We're the good guys everyone is looking for. I sold the Hercules. . .'

'What next, then, Auric?' Masha asks. 'Could you be my sister? Most everyone is exiled now – everyone I've known. Will the rest be generous? It's changing, Auric – are you aware?'

'I have a problem with you, Masha,' Auric says. 'Religion is the big thing now – people will die for it, and not much else. That doesn't interest you. The little states – they're gasping. Will you still remain a founding symbol there? Where shall we go, who'll take us now?'

'There's Delia,' says Masha. 'Regina, even. I could walk the world, explore Brazil. . . Of course, they will have changed. . .'

'It all has changed,' says Auric, showing her a clip. 'Things don't last long like they used to – people have nine lives, when one is lost, you have to change your skin. . .' There's Auric on a tiny screen, limbering towards an orgy – there's the disc, Deep Amber, you can't see or hear what's on it, but there's nudes in masks around, and drumming – 'You could enrol yourself, Masha,' Auric says, as the scene unscrolls. 'You know all about yourself, most people now are dead, not even proper fascists – when we made the video, we were high on maraschino and some pills. . . And after, I went breaking things – some guys from Chad. . .'

They're in a car, there's dripping letters – 'Declaring independence'. 'Of course,' says Auric, wiping tears, 'That was all long ago. They're all in their sixties or their seventies now. . .'

'It looks like fun, I guess,' says Masha. 'But – the maraschino, doesn't sound much class.'

'Oh,' says Auric. 'It's the sugar rush. You don't get over it, not in your lifetime. When you die they plant you with a hive on top – out grow the sweetest things, your bones – like candy sticks. . .'

'I didn't want the power,' says Masha. 'Having to dress good, make those jokes. Then – there's the cadavers, you get used to them, but you can't say you have, and maybe you must draw a bead on someone for yourself – like hunting on the pier, in a glass box you see the mandarin, you press your button and he's yours, except it isn't done to hang him on your wall. . . That is philosophy as well, dear Auric, and now you do it in the real, over and over, the puzzle's always there, though you forget it. . .'

'Yes, yes, I know,' says Auric, looking at himself some years ago, waving a rubber pizzle, grinning, spinning on one leg like Rumpelstiltskin. . . 'You're not a zealot or a chief for very long, and you don't read the book, but while you're up, you must believe! – without sincerity, it all falls in a heap. . . Yes, Masha, I know that's only a part of it. Nothing dies – it proliferates but splits into tiny simulacra – there's millions of Hitlers now – they do no harm, they're shrimps by the bucketload. It all goes on and on – they become our germs, our viruses – we catch one, any one, you never know – and shortly – it goes away, or we die: some with a bomb tied to our gut. If you're a musician – you know all that. The material is so simple – we humans don't hear much. Those in the forest with good ears – they don't sing too loud – frightens the animals. The rest – a coupla octaves, being a faun, singing in the waterfall . . . we music guys, we can all play everything and make you cry. Or march in step. It's very, very simple – you just need be good at it – like wrapping cream cakes in a paper. Not everybody can.'

*

'We have money,' Auric says. 'That means we can leave this room. It's when the two of us are poor and stuck together.'

'What then?' asks Masha, much alarmed. 'You're small. . . '

'But strong,' says Auric, 'and pissed off. We could have had much more. You have in mind, Masha, to be far and wee. Those elms – they sway. Those rooks scream all night with the fear. This room's secure – you think it's jail, but no, it protects. . .'

'I feel I must get away somewhere,' Masha says. 'Not round the block.'

'The cash is mine,' says Auric, stretching out.

'Don't threaten,' Masha says. 'It's not a sitting room with family, minor officials, manuscripts in a drawer.'

'It's clearly a stretching room,' says Auric. 'And no

one shoots themselves, or anybody else in the next room. There isn't one.'

'I couldn't hit you, Auric, however you provoke,' says Masha. 'Never again the leaves unfurl, the chrysalis that cracks. . . '

'Don't worry,' Auric says. 'I'm not a visual type. And I know all the tunes. I don't think that they'd be missed.'

'Did you sell the club, the bat, that Hercules was hefting?' Masha asks.

'No. That's for another plot,' he says. 'Be sure, I'll follow you if you run off. If I feel like it, of course. I have the cash. . .'

'I like the centre,' Masha says, 'or the outside – this is a suburb. It's closed in – that's not been my problem in the past. I don't trust the neighbours – some steal cars, and others don't. It's quite too complicated – everyone's involved, in one way or another.'

She makes the baseball bat sing in the air. He's right – it's very small, you'd need some expertise to kill a lion, or any other thing.

She tells Auric, 'You're a great criminal, a great thief: a murderer, an informer. You've impoverished my life.'

'No, Masha,' he says, lying on the Chesterfield, looking good, relaxed. 'You impoverished mine. Those so casual, well-trained guys, top guns – they could have hit you with their bombs back home; their rockets. Or you could have fucked yourself – you had the chance. Drowned, starved, dropped off your branch. It seems you're immortal, Masha, you're the bad smell that comes from tombs.'

*

'He was fine when I left him,' Masha says, and she waves the brick of notes.

'Delia!' It can't be her. she's small, her face screwed like a nut, there's a dreadful shade of pink, health all over. 'I've so much to say,' says Masha. 'I can't remember half of it.'

'Your Russian family?' asks Delia.

'Oh no,' says Masha. 'I took the name – remember, we all did, they bombed so hard. And then I found myself with intellectuals, gamekeepers, customs men . . . so, I felt I ought to make a trip. Realise myself. . .'

'That's what we did,' Delia says. 'We have a toucan sanctuary, Regina and I. We're kissing sisters,' she stumbles, the words don't trip easy. . .

'I thought toucans only did publicity,' Masha says.

'Oh yes, they do,' says Delia. 'That's where the money is. They're in the spirit. With their broken wings.'

'You seem much smaller, Delia,' Masha says.

'What joy!' says Delia. 'You saw. We're all going back to our original size, we in the forest. When we're a metre high, we're neat, we're not molested.'

'I'm sure they'll hunt you,' Masha says, at a loss.

'Oh,' Delia says. 'There's plants and amulets that keep you safe.'

'The ones who roasted Ben? Who took the path of enlightenment. . . ' asks Masha.

'Getting on for three metres high,' says Delia. 'They need a lot of fuel.'

'I'm not sure I'd fit in either way,' Masha says. 'I'm stuck, in the middle size.'

'You have a sense of justice, Masha,' Delia says. 'Being wronged, wanting justice, doing it, not doing it. That's why you're stuck. You're not at ease, not with yourself, nor with the past.'

'But, I don't feel just,' says Masha, quite desperate.

'I'm sure you aren't, Masha,' Delia says. 'Why would you be? How can anyone be? Give it up, my dear.'

'And come with you?' asks Masha timidly.

'Oh no, I never said,' says Delia. 'We say no to priests and anthro guys, tax collectors and the humanists. Another sister – would be incongruous. Though of course we love you. I do – Regina can't stand you. We fear you, too. You're, well – too big.'

Masha weeps. She's had enough of forests – dense ones – but seeing tears, Delia'll feel bad.

'A donation's always welcome,' Delia says. 'And your news was so exciting.'

Delia hugs Masha's knees. Masha lays her hands on her head. 'I shan't be back,' says Delia. 'They give us primitives a hard time at the borders.'

*

It's a dreadful thing, Masha thinks, to lose a sister. It should be worse to lose whole populations, a culture, notables and stars – a landslide falling on your village, your town bombed, disproportionately.

When you're alone, she thinks, you think of your defence. Your threat – if it's not to be a bluff that's called – you have to mean it thoroughly. If you're not determined – better not go armed. If you've a knife – your enemy will have a gun. If you've a gun – she'll have two, a mate to back her up. No matter. Don't fool with them. Always face off from strength. Don't think of some defensive ploy – that just invites attack. You must be ready to act first, eliminate. You'll find some off-key guys, lodged in a bar – they'll tell you to attack, to be convinced – it's an important truth, it saves your life, not someone else's. And as for sentiment, regret – the more go down, the easier it becomes, she thinks; that's comforting, it's contralogical.

'I'll miss you, Delia,' Masha thinks, though she can't know.

*

'You're abstracted,' says the lady, the stranger. A proud walker on the earth. Clearly she has a mother tongue, firm behind her teeth; a favourite store for buying her pro clothes. She could be in psychiatry, immigration – some kind of borderline control. Of course – she might be recruiting girlie ninjas, her partner blueblack with grunge tattoos waiting stoned around the corner.

'Oh,' Masha says, 'not me, I'm quite concrete – maybe my former friend left me with a troubled brow. . . He's in good health, resting, on his Chesterfield. A personality problem – he was into music, that way you don't have a nation and its language . . . nor all the rest – values, a personal number you must carry to the grave. . . It's universal script and sounds – they drift over frontiers and the hills. . .'

'If you're troubled,' says the lady, Irene she's called. 'What you do is not accountable.'

'It means I can do anything,' says Masha, who already knows all that.

'You can't do anything,' the lady says. 'There is no you.'

It's casuistry, but Irene goes on, 'Though – of course, you can have sisters.'

'What do you propose, Irene?' asks Masha. 'Life is just one person, then another generation, following like flights of china ducks upon a dreary wall.'

'What a banality, dear Masha,' says Irene, quite shocked. 'You need a shakeup. Science, nature, brothers, artefacts – I *thought* you'd been around abstractions far too long. Even sisters – if you don't move on – they stay in bobbysox, with braces on their teeth . . . .'

'I've done everything,' says Masha. 'I'm waiting for no train. I don't care who shoots himself in the next room. I don't point, and I don't chum.'

'I really think that's so,' says Irene, admiring. 'You're not terrorised, I see.'

'No,' Masha says. 'Any fear I have, it comes from me.'

'You've worn the veil,' Irene says. 'And that's all past. The new – you don't pine for it, I see, nor think there's value in the past. . .'

'Oh,' Masha says. 'Maybe there is, but it's all dirty

stuff, and I can't puff, or sell. Old men, new men, sisters of all genres – well, all men are brothers, naturally. But – in those words I find no light.'

'Excellent!' Irene says. 'We'll get on fine. My creed is – eat the fruit, chop down the tree. No one knows quite where they want to go, nor where they've been. I see everything so clear!'

'Yes, yes!' shouts Masha. 'That's me too!'

'I've been everywhere,' Irene says, 'and I took notes. Wrote it all down. The slums – are cosy, but they flood. The tented cities – aah, the sandstorms, and the scorpions in your socks. There's Edens, naturally, with water and an export trade. But envy! Masha dear – maybe it's for betterment. I don't want to end on losing sides. But – the winning ones – they don't appeal. Often too – they haven't lasted. I'm not a humanist, of course – who could go back there? Those Petrarch sonnets, ink wet still, off the press. . . But – you don't win and you don't lose . . . if you don't deal . . . what are you then? Graffiti? My problem is – I don't like holes – the dark, the underground. Nor heights – the swaying. And the rooks.'

'Those are my conclusions too,' says Masha, 'but there's no curtain to come down and have the people say "how wise", and leave.'

'Oh Masha,' Irene says. 'You're so adorable! If only

. . . I could have a sister just like you. Not even like – a copy, replica. You wouldn't say it was a fake.'

'The surface could be real – the underneath – not quite authentic,' Masha says.

'Oh let's not think about authenticity – that ramp!' Irene says. 'They're real – that is enough – the past was real for sure, and so the future must be too. If you're my sister I acquire your past and future – and I put you in my bag, you're another of my ginseng roots. . .' and Masha peers down: there's notebooks – all the places Irene's been to, didn't wish to stay – and ginseng roots, brown and lucent like netsuke. . .

'I love your bag,' says Masha, not sincere – Irene ignores her – even the devil has his sack. . .

'I travelled round,' Irene says. 'My reasoning went with the clouds, when there were some, or with the winds, the grit, the smells – the papers and the parchments blown in heaps. . . You know, my dear – they save the lions, and there's so many cubs they're sent to parks and then get shot for cash that goes to save the lions. . . People get driven out – you'd need to give them guns, instead they put them into tents and squalor, and resent the cost. . .'

'Yes, yes,' says Masha. 'We've all heard all that. It's not part of our universe, Irene, it's a scene that we avoid.

We're young and running still – you stop, and there's a paradox like poison ivy round your legs. . .'

'You don't find a paradox in nature,' Irene says. 'Only in figures – figures of speech . . . not on scrolls, not in a raga. I told you – I'm not a sympathetic type, I don't get horrified – just uncomfortable.'

'Oh, I agree,' says Masha, 'I'm a moderate myself,' and she waves her stump: 'Hot, cold, mould. . . Discomfort – that's what dictates. Think of those antelopes on the Tibetan plain – they can't cross railroad tracks and highways. No one could. They're nothing much to look at – you can't say I'm sentimental, that I want one in my yard. You help them – see! They're grateful. . . '

'Oh gardens, plants!' says Irene, laughing. 'They grow so high! God must have had a gardener to prune the plums. . .'

'We were told,' says Masha, 'that light was different in those days – located lower down. Maybe it rose up from cut stones – the diamonds scattered in the grass. . . Quite useless then, without a goldsmith, and of course the guys to mine the stuff. . .'

'Let's be modest,' says Irene. 'Deal with what we have before us, not what happens when the last couple's left, before extinction. Will they be two gays, I wonder?

That would satisfy aesthetics – there'd be one left in any case. . . Maybe that shows it's all the same. One left – who didn't write it down, and no one left to read – of course, there could be scattered hundreds left, leaving no records, giving up on kids. . .'

'Irene!' shouts Masha. 'Leave that meander! Do not speculate! That's not in nature. . . Onward! That's the word. We need to find our tempo, pool what we know, and then set out, together, possibly. You're a poet, Irene, I haven't trekked with one of those – remember, your fancy clouds your insight. . .' She thinks of Gritt, Auric, Duval – no poet there, but Ben? Perhaps, perhaps.

'Oh, I'll rein it in,' Irene says. 'Some say imagination leads to power – not that I want it – but I'll tell you, naked, what I see.'

Here they are – this big empty house in trees. . . 'I didn't know how rich you were, Irene,' says Masha.

'Oh no,' Irene says, 'I didn't pay a cent. It's empty now – until we go inside, of course. . .' she laughs. 'There's everything you'd need. Here,' and she lifts a bead curtain, 'is nature.'

There can't be parrots, monkeys, flitting round among the plants – they'd starve – but you might daub them in, in imagination, if you'd a commission for a pastiche of an old engraving, a sketchpad left awaiting rediscovery –

like Cuba, till those caravelles – isle untouched but lively for millennia. . . 'Here,' Irene says, twirling a metal wheel to open an iron door, 'is nurture.'

There's a bench, some gas taps. 'Of course,' says Masha. 'The leaves, the figs, the nuts, the crimson tongues – nature! You'd be an idiot to choose the lab!'

'Exactly, Masha,' says Irene. 'I'd lounge in nature all day long – except, it's a shame not to twiddle something out of nurture. . . Masha – that's your heritage. Nothing will come of it, I'm sure: just stinks and flashes: I'm an optimist! You'll be like Doctor Gritt, you'll save the world, and then another plague, a flail, a scythe long two kilometres – will force you into new discoveries. . . It's not my thing. You'll save the world and get the plaudit – me, I'll stretch out in the sun and eat those figs.'

'Oh dear,' says Masha. 'I hope this isn't just a metaphor, this house: free will, and faith, and primal gifts from some invisible deity, a Pan demanding sacrifice and practice on those goddam pipes, concerts where no one comes, Hell's Angels on a ramp, all that. . .'

'No, no, my dear,' Irene says. 'Here there's no metaphors, nor paradox. It's all clean stuff. The horrors stay outside – there's just us two, bound in our sisterhood. From the air, the trees will hide us: no bombardments and no requisitioning, no refugees, no squaddies looking for some love, no zealots trying to convert. . . The only thing – is if the guys who built or bought the house, and now are absent – try to come back in. We'll have to fight them off. But with some luck – they'll have forgotten the address, been jailed or blasted, enrolled, become ascetics – and we shan't need these guns, the rockets here. . .' And she shows Masha a bright set of tubes, 'Call this Stalin's organ – maybe it was Molotov's,' she says. 'One does forget . . . for sure, they're not the pipes of Pan,' and they both laugh.

'One last thing,' Irene says. 'Before you wash the bottles out and start to pour and weigh. If I were you, dear Masha, though we're sisters, that bond eternal, indissoluble – I wouldn't trust me. I know your secrets – you've no idea what mine might be.'

'Oh, I don't care,' says Masha. 'If you steal what I invent – see! I have no index, I can't indicate direction. No hither, so no thither. What comes out of my imagination – it's from altruism and the random. . . I have no title . . . not to anything. I'm just like you, squatting in this house. Property's not only theft, it's clear: it isn't efficacious. The guys who used this place – they didn't rest on law and documents – they left this rocket launcher. . . '

No!' shouts Irene. 'Don't touch that knob! You'll give

away our presence, break the windows too. . .'

*

'Well, dear,' Irene calls. 'What have you invented? Discovered, I mean, of course. I'm polishing Voroshilov's organ – is that right? You'd know the name. Maybe some stuffed birds in here – would make you feel at home?'

'I've explained all that, Irene,' says Masha. 'So, no! I uncovered an inexhaustible free fuel – we used it, journeying in the balloon. Auric was the brawn. But someone had an earlier claim. Afflatus, it was named. Now, I'm thinking about food. From nothing, Irene. . .'

'Oh Masha – that's been done,' Irene says. 'It grows all round. From less than naught. Myself – I use the fridge. But when that's done, you wouldn't need the basket. There's figs and nuts, and eggs from parrots – other kinds of flying things as well. It's protein, Masha, like in beans, but crawls and stings. That door is open, dear – don't push it more. Try for something less grand, Masha: something to whisk the dust off leaves. . .'

'I'm an ambitious type, Irene,' says Masha. 'But – your rockets – might it smack of overkill?'

'Oh,' Irene says, squeezing Masha. 'It's just

deterrence. The guys that were here before – they're maybe bigots, oafs. Not us. We need a place to think, invent, relax. A haven.'

'Oh yes, Irene,' says Masha, quite sincere. 'I know you keep me safe, and that you love me too. . . But – might I ask a thing? Don't lock that door, don't lock me in. I'll work, so there's no need. . .'

'You want a contract, dear?' Irene asks. They laugh. 'It's just my little tic, my dear, to keep you safe. If those guys come back, through the side door. . .'

'I have to keep a window open,' Masha says. 'Unless I just work on some equation . . . you need some paper, ink, a slate . . . that's all, you close the window, and that's it.'

'You can rest up,' Irene says. 'In the sun lounge – but it's a waste. You'd be a parasite. You don't need two to keep the rockets bright. . .'

'Equations,' Masha says. 'They're quiet, don't smell. You can keep the windows closed. But – they're dull. Something equals something else – it turns out they're identical.'

'That isn't it at all,' Irene says. 'You find two disparate things – you place them in your frame – it turns out, when you tweak them, that they are the same. That's comradeship, fraternity. It's dull, for sure – but think of it as metamorphoses. What you see is something else as well. The egg plus nest – is eagle. And so on.'

'I can do all that,' says Masha. 'I'd just need some chalk. But – so what. I'd sooner save the world than find we're twirling in a monstrous space that's full of rushing things invisible and lumpish. . . But after that – I could come in with you, Irene, all day! Lie in the sun, true lounge lizards two!'

'No, no,' Irene says. 'Our love respects the other's distance. Their talent.'

'Well, Irene,' Masha asks. 'What is your vision?'

Irene says firmly, 'Keeping you safe, my dear. Making sure the territory outside is clear – that no militiamen, no gardeners, ostlers, coachmen, tweenies – anything you choose to give a function to – is lurking there, by the side door, ready to storm in, to do us down . . . That's why I have to lock you in, dear Masha. If we start parleying with all the guys outside – we'd never end. Our choice is tough – you fight, or run. You can't trust those who want to come inside – there is no movement, nothing of the 'left' political, if that's what you are thinking of. You cannot share, cut deals, with all that crowd. It's finished, everywhere. Capital's the thing, it is our air and water – if we should pierce the azure canopy above, out they would seep . . . and we'd be dinosaurs, dear Masha. Even the rich have given up – they don't fear socialism – they only fear the end. I'm your protection, Masha. Your Doctor Gritt gave us our energy, free and infinite. We're humming like a hornet's disco – even the planet spins and hops, it's polka time, those saxes are red hot – until . . . I'm sure you've been there in your mind, dear Masha. The end.'

'Oh yes, Irene,' says Masha, 'I've been there many times. There's nothing new to come for me. Long long ago, women wanted to get out, to take the little train, a ticket to the city, freedom, cash, revolution even – then, the disappointment when you found the doors were locked!'

'I know.' Irene says. 'It seems you know as well. Go back inside, and do your task, my love.'

'They say that occupying places like we have – it isn't just the hassling and the pillage. It stresses you. Those Germans had some luck – if they had won their war, they would have suffered terribly. The massacres come back and bite you on the toe . . . even if you've deities behind you,' Masha says.

'That's history,' says Irene, 'that's why no one can make it out, the past – allot the blame. This old weapon here,' and she pats the launcher. 'Who else but me can arm it, remember all those ancient names? I'm the good guy now, my dear, I'll take the stress, I can't do less.'

She locks Masha in the lab. Masha'd quite like to save the world. She isn't good at maths, she wavers, blurs, the stick of chalk snaps off – maybe her head is lightening up – there's gas – a leak. . . Up in the balloon – there you feel free, she thinks. Duval, Auric – they were coarse, but fun. . .

There's shapes that flitter in the park. Irene thinks the pipes would make a tingling, whistling sound. . . She says a prayer to Pan – she'd like to set the rockets off. Then – Music ho!

'It's old stuff,' Masha says. 'Weapons. Once, it liberates, then it's sold. There's maybe other arms upstairs – they have no nationality, Irene. It's trade. It's liquid, flows all round. Everything is easy now, it's fluid – on your desk, you press a key – there's all the ideas there's ever been, and bios too of every guy who's out there, hiding behind the trees. . .'

'Back to your work!' Irene says. 'We know all that. This organ's what I'm left with. It's old, it works. . . So, Masha, what's the new, where you say you're coming from? In olden times, there were the mysteries, the things that everybody thought they knew but didn't talk about. Now, Masha, forget the orchards and the birds – discover the last secret, we'll cash in, and then. . .'

'Oh, it's not so difficult,' says Masha. 'It's rockets. Bigger than an ark; faster than eagles. . . Up to the stars, Irene! But that trip is not for me. I've run. I've lied about my origins. Just to survive! Now, I don't want to leave, to start an empire somewhere you can't see, but possibly it twinkles – far, far up there. . .'

'I knew! I knew!' Irene shouts. 'Rockets! I thought it! It's a disappointment, this epiphany, but still . . . Rockets – destroy the bad guys, lift the good guys up, to start again! A new Siberia, to colonise. . .'

They're not enthusiastic, not for long. Masha's discovery – it disappoints. The lab is stark. And yet, there's comfort here, the sun lounge lets you sleep and dream – of cockatoos; ripe mangoes dangling round your head. . .

'Maybe I'll just stay and fight them off, the gardeners,' says Irene. 'You, Masha – wipe the equation off the board. You maybe got a squiggle wrong. It wouldn't work.'

'You mean, Irene,' says Masha, 'this is it, the whole? The *arcana*? Heaven, paradise. Baggage limits: 'you can't take it with you' . . . 'lay not treasures up on Earth, you're leaving now' . . . The fiery chariots, annunciations . . . the prequel, was that it?'

'You can't say we weren't informed,' says Irene.

'Alas, it's so banal . . . and quite uncertain. How does the grand story end? Maybe it doesn't, but for you and me, Masha, it does. The last line – who wants to say it? The curtain falls, stagehands depart, the obligatory fireman puts his helmet in its box. . . We disappear. . .'

'You already know the plot,' says Masha. 'If you've a trilogy in mind. Father, son – and lastly sister – each tiptoes across the quicksands or the coals – and meets a tragic end. . . It shan't be us, Irene! My equation – means a change of scene, but nothing more. The ancient drama doesn't change.'

'I think you knew already, dear,' says Irene. 'In the balloon. Ever upward, rising from tree to cloud. . . A new planet – with those same old plays. Now – do as I say – rub the equation out. 'Heavy weights and shortened time, somehow equals distance.' My! It's quite beyond me, Masha. . . We'd be lifted up by Gritt – his resolution, his resolve . . . his energy. You believed that there were barriers, a universe designed by logic, with stable properties. . . All overcome, it seems – and yet – repeated further on.'

'If we *all* go,' Masha says, 'up, I mean, things'll be the same, once each has found a place to sit. If only some – us, probably – are left, what's different?'

'Exactly, Masha,' says Irene. 'The design's the same.

The epic thrust is constant. Our species plays out the plot identical, established right from the start. Two actors, maybe three: the Furies, or the Persians, Thebans maybe, they assail, then there's revenge, disloyalty, comeuppance. . . Justice as massacre: the ending always is the same, contrived. We can't all die at once, can we, my dear? It shouldn't be for us. We're sisters. Stay off the stage, Masha, if you can – it's all a con. We're happy here, my love, aren't we?' she asks: 'Think back. Remember where you came from. This, what we have now – this is the best. "Polish your rockets, eliminate the bad; and what remains is good."'

Masha doesn't see it so. 'The organ, Irene – the pipes – it's rather scattershot,' she says.

'It's quite precise,' Irene shouts, angrily. 'You need lots of missiles since there's lots of bad. Each bang's exact. Besides – who cares? The bad guys go far back, centuries, millennia . . . what do you expect? Better stuff? Conversions?'

*

Masha's task – completed. She moves in to the lounge, with Irene. She has her own daybed, a bowl of cherries too.

‘Those who go to space,’ Irene says, ‘they’d need to take a big idea – or else it wouldn’t be the new. . .’

‘We who are left,’ says Masha, ‘defend. We can have happiness. Sisterhood. Even – brotherhood. But that big idea, Irene, is credit. Universal. Banks. It used to be the Plan. Those who’re shot up – up to the stars – that’s what they’ll take. . .’

‘Oh,’ Irene laughs. ‘Masha! You’re so snide and cynical! Left-handed! Is that your take? On everything? Come over here, by me, come for a cuddle, dear.’

And she does.

About the author

John Fraser has lived in Rome since 1980. Previously, he worked in England and Canada.

www.ingramcontent.com/pod-product-compliance
Lightning Source LLC
Chambersburg PA
CBHW020549310726
48979CB00008B/1142/J

* 9 7 8 1 9 1 0 3 0 1 3 8 8 *